[*Aliens of Affection*

Also by Padgett Powell

Edisto (1984)

A Woman Named Drown (1987)

Typical (1991)

Edisto Revisited (1996)

[*Aliens of Affection*

stories by Padgett Powell   ]

Henry Holt and Company

New York

Henry Holt and Company, Inc.
Publishers since 1866
115 West 18th Street
New York, New York 10011

Henry Holt® is a registered trademark of
Henry Holt and Company, Inc.

Stories in this collection have previously appeared in *Harper's,
Esquire, BOMB, DoubleTake, The Paris Review,
Gettysburg Review, New England Review, The Chattahoochee Review,*
and *Mississippi Review.*

Library of Congress Cataloging-in-Publication Data
Powell, Padgett.
Aliens of affection : stories / by Padgett Powell. —1st ed.
p.   cm.
ISBN 0-8050-5213-5 (acid-free paper)
I. Title.
PS3566.08328A79   1998
813'.54—dc21   97-10451

Henry Holt books are available for special promotions and
premiums. *For details contact:* Director, Special Markets.

First Edition 1998

Designed by Cynthia Krupat

An Editor's Press Book: Pat Strachan

Printed in the United States of America
All first editions are printed on acid-free paper. ∞

10   9   8   7   6   5   4   3   2   1

For Sidney

On account of the fact, he said gentlemanly, that I have at all times purposely refrained from an exhaustive exercise of my faculty of vision and my power of optical inspection (I refer now to things perfectly palpable and discernible—the coming of dawn across the mountains is one example and the curious conduct of owls and bats in strong moonlight is another), I had expected (foolishly, perhaps), that I should be able to see quite clearly things that are normally not visible at all as a compensation for my sparing inspection of the visible.

—Flann O'Brien, *At Swim-Two-Birds*

Contents

[*Trick or Treat*

[**O**n her way to the grocery store, to which she could walk, in celebration of which she often wore lizard-skin cowboy boots and other dress excessive for a daily trip to buy food for a family, Mrs. Hollingsworth recited, "It loves me, it loves me not. I love *it,* I love it not—" until she was interrupted by a child behind a picket fence next to the sidewalk.

"What are you talking about, lady?" This came equably from a round freckled face just above the sharpened pickets, all of which suggested briefly an uncarved, unlit pumpkin speaking to her.

"The South," Mrs. Hollingsworth said to the pumpkin face, which she presumed, not altogether comfortably, a portrait of innocence. The child was in fact a portrait of insolence and had wanted to say not "What are you talking about, lady?" but "Hey, lady, how about some pussy?" He had watched her for weeks walk in costumes to and from the store and he had prodigious twelve-year-old need.

"The South?" he asked. "What's that?"

"This," Mrs. Hollingsworth said, indicating with her arm the trees and air and houses and suspiring history and ennui and corruption and meanness and game violators and bottomland and chivalric humanism and people who are smart about money and people who don't have a clue and heroism and stray pets around them.

"Have you lost your mind?" the boy asked.

Mrs. Hollingsworth, to whom the proposition was tenable, said, "Grow up," and walked on.

The child was left there in a rage of early tumescence, kicking himself for insulting the object of his waking and sleeping lusts. The back of his T-shirt, which Mrs. Hollingsworth had not seen, said JUST BLOW ME, ostensibly in promotion of a brand of bubble gum. He had had the wit not to let his parents see the shirt and knew, almost, what it meant. He had the mouth and the *where* right but was taking the BLOW literally. He had intended asking Mrs. Hollingsworth how about some pussy and then turning his back to her. It would have worked, he was sure.

The child had no way of knowing that it *would* probably have worked. Mrs. Hollingsworth had three children, one older than her suitor, and had been happily married for fifteen years, and was a good mother and wife, and was enraged about it. She had said recently to a business associate of her husband, who had been out of town and had appointed her the associate's entertainment in his stead, which associate had begun kissing the back of her neck in the car outside the restaurant she'd taken them to, "Hey, for all you know, I might be the town tramp." What the business associate thought of her and her proclivities, if anything, is not known; he kept kissing her neck, which she proffered more of, and angled her head to make taut and handsome.

What Mrs. Hollingsworth thought was: I *could be* the town tramp. The business associate was, in fact, not the first relief she had had from the happy marriage, but she had not entertained the notion of going wholesale. She would have entertained the notion of this little smart-ass pumpkin head, *un* Lolito. It was hysterical, she was hysterical, it was perfect. But the pumpkin head had not shown his cards.

The next time Mrs. Hollingsworth saw the child he was standing on her front stoop with a new-looking Lawn-Boy mower behind him the color of a katydid. Through the peephole's fish-eye lens the boy looked obscenely older, his freckles the size of rain splats on concrete, and the mower was giving off shafts of a soft green light that was spectral.

She opened the door and said, neutrally, "Yes?" and looked from the boy to the mower and back to the boy and then up and down the boy.

"What?" he said. "My shorts?" He looked down at his shorts, which were cutoffs with ridiculously lacerated hems. In fact, she saw then, they had been sliced up from the cut edge about two inches on about one-inch centers, giving them a kind of surrey-roof frill. His skinny legs hung out of this frilliness like strings themselves. Mrs. Hollingsworth laughed and said, "No, not your shorts."

"What, then?"

"*What* what?"

"What are you laughing at?"

"I'm not laughing."

"You were too."

Mrs. Hollingsworth laughed again.

"See?"

She laughed some more.

"Goddamn, lady."

"What?"

"*What* what," he said, obviously mocking her.

"Goddamn what?"

"Just *goddamn*, lady."

"Okay. That's better."

The boy drew himself up, as if in summary of certain points he had been making. "Do you want your lawn cut?" When he said this, a hail of profane words and images fell in his brain. Do you want a cherry on it? Do you want nuts on it? Do you want your nuts crushed? Do you want your tits blown off? "Do you want your lawn cut?" he said again, strangely almost out of breath.

"No," Mrs. Hollingsworth said. "But you can cut it anyway."

She closed the door then and decided that would be the test for this little rogue: if he cut the lawn with no more ado, no price, no terms, no promise, he was to be regarded as a significant little foul ball landing in the happy proper play of her enraging days.

Through the fish-eyed peephole Mrs. Hollingsworth watched him address his Lawn-Boy. He took a deep breath and glanced at the sky before securing the machine with his foot and pulling the cord. It started right up. He took the handle and pushed against it with his thighs, stood there not moving, and momentarily seemed to wilt over the handle before taking a giant stride. He marched the machine over the lawn faster than she had ever seen a lawn mower go. He was flying over the lawn, blasting sticks and ant beds and, he thought, a pet toy of some sort into flakbursts of airborne detritus that was collecting around his nostrils. He was a cute little thing.

When she let him into the back yard and he did not talk or even look at her, Mrs. Hollingsworth confirmed her suspicions that the child was on a sexual mission. He was bold and terrified.

"I'll make the lemonade," she said.

He said, "Yes'm."

Not "make us some lemonade," not "Would you like some lemonade, or something?" *The* lemonade. She was thrilled by this little stage irony. The boy was not himself unaware of something off. "Yes'm" was as close as he had ever come in his life to saying "ma'am."

When he finished the blitzkrieg of the yard, he sat on the little two-seater rowing swing on the children's gym set and Mrs. Hollingsworth emerged with a tray. On it was a hand-painted pitcher and tumblers and loose lemons as garnish—impractical but irresistible to Mrs. Hollingsworth's sense of kitsch in still life. She noted how unadult the boy looked sitting where her own children sat, even though he was obviously consumed with adult concerns. She wondered for the first time why he was not, as her children were, in school.

She put the tray on one seat of the glider, also attached to the gym set, though it was clearly intended for adults. It was a swinging double-benched arbor, actually, and her plan was to sit them both on one of the benches opposite the lemonade and serve the child properly until the accidental touch, or his blurting whatever he might blurt, set the lunacy of his early need and her late fatigue in motion.

Before any of this was effected, they heard the crackle of a police radio and Mrs. Hollingsworth saw, over the gate of the wooden fence through which she had let the boy, the cap and face of a police officer. He said, in a preposterously deep-voiced tone of authority, "What's going on here?"

"We're having *lemonade* in the *shade*, Officer," Mrs. Hollingsworth managed, attempting with her emphases—unsuccessfully, she knew—to insult the policeman.

"Who?" he said.

"Whose business—" Mrs. Hollingsworth noticed that the boy was gone. In a decimated patch of earth beside the glider there was a deep, lugged sneaker print pointed in the direction of the back fence. She could imagine a blur of surrey frill and skinny leg going over her good six-foot redwood fence. The image made her inexplicably, inordinately fond of her little charge, though suspicious of this rather simple affection for insouciance, or whatever it was that made a boy escape authority and made authority—in this case, herself— like it. She could also not help thinking, as the officer rather brazenly let himself through the gate, *sex with cops.* He came up, a shiny-shoed flashing noisy navy-blue binding of regulations and procedure.

"Have a look at that lawn mower, ma'am?"

Mrs. Hollingsworth gave him permission, which he did not wait for, with a wave of her hand. She was observing things she had no real time to observe without giving the officer the impression that she was spacey. She did not care; it was, after all, the police. The kid was right. She thought of "things." How, of late, she had begun to like the idea of losing her mind. That was the conventional expression for it, not hers. She was toying with the idea of losing herself. She did not want her mind to depart, like the whole house of one's Kansas spinning to Oz; she wanted the little craft of things that were considered *her*, that she considered her, to work loose and drift and turn just a little off-line, a keelless rowboat about 45 degrees to the current in a gentle, non-threatening high water. The officer was telling her, standing before her and mincing as if he had to go somewhere or pee, that the lawn mower had been stolen from the hardware store eight blocks away by a boy on foot.

"Get your plaster, Officer."

"Ma'am?"

"Here's his track."

"The alleged individual who perpetrated was in the apparel of a shirt of the variety of a T-shirt which it had printed on it an obscene . . . ah, saying. Or remark." This speech endeared the officer to Mrs. Hollingsworth in a way that surprised her, but she caught herself. If she was going to have immoral affections for a Lolito, she was not going to accommodate Sergeant García. She had no idea what the obscene-shirt business was about. The boy had had on a clean white shirt. That was the only true thing she told the officer about the boy.

"The alleged perpetrator, Officer, had dark skin, though he wasn't black or Hispanic, and he did not seem too bright, but I wouldn't go so far as to say he was mentally challenged." The officer wrote things in a fold-over pocket-sized spiral notebook.

"He had on mordantly long pants."

"What?"

"Mordantly long pants."

"Can you describe those pants?"

"Mordant."

"Oh."

The Bee Gees were playing, filling the yard. She had put them on, and put a speaker in a window giving on the back yard, for the lemonade break. Even she knew they were terribly dated, that the boy would either find them hokey in modern terms or not even know what disco was, and that had been part of the scheme: to look agreeable but hopelessly out of it to the boy. It would give him a certain courage, perhaps the courage of pity or charity. Now, sitting there, she thought she could see the officer just perceptibly dancing as he pulled the evidence of her suitor's crime out of the yard. And she sat there herself not unhappily in a flood of harmonized sappiness that not even a teenager should tolerate. The rowboat of her self was coming unmoored, perhaps, inch by inch.

She wondered how disruptive to the courtship this unfortunate incident would prove until, an hour later, she picked up the phone and heard a voice coming through what sounded like a pillow say, "Bonnie? This is Clyde. Rain check on that lemonade," and the caller hang up giggling. She had a card on her hands and she was going to have to decide if she really was one herself. To do that, you had to look boredom in the eye and forget all other considerations: your own failures contributing to your boredom, for example. Does God, you had to ask, want us to be bored? You answer that to find out if you are a card or not. You do not entertain highfalutin notions of decadence. Just *boredom.* That is to some extent what the kid was operating on, that and hormones, even though he didn't know it (he knew the hormones, but not boredom as such, yet, she figured). In his early apprehension of boredom boring down on him, he was arguably a little visionary, if you took the long, charitable view of him. If you took the short, niggardly view, he was a young dog with a blue steel. Her husband came home shortly after these thoughts and Mrs. Hollingsworth took the long, charitable view of the boy.

—

Her husband lugged his business-day you-wouldn't-believe-it opera of sigh and grunt into the house and she gave him the kiss to make it all better. This kiss, on the cheek, had a special feature: she touched the back of his neck with the back of her left hand while holding his arm, at the biceps, with her right hand. For the implantation of this ministration her husband held perfectly still so that the target, his cheek, would be steady. The kiss had originated, she supposed, from her having wet her hands doing dishes and not wanting to wet her husband. But she had noticed that it was now the only way she would kiss him; she would touch him only with the back of her hand. It had become a symbol of her dissatisfaction. She thought of kissing the boy: taking his little fine-haired neck with her hand and fingers up into his hair, cradling the little pumpkin properly, and kissing him as tenderly or roughly as he seemed to suggest movies and television had taught him he wanted to be kissed. She might take his face in *both* hands, if he inclined to tenderness and innocence. She might turn his head, even, like a listening puppy's. She might move her lips seductively and ridiculously, as Marilyn Monroe did, before actually kissing him. She realized at dinner—meat loaf with Lipton Onion Soup Mix in it, they'd have it no other way—that her affair with this rogue lawn boy was as unknowable a thing as anything available to her in her life as it stood, and as it was ever likely to stand. As silly or sad as it was, it was possible to regard entertaining the boy and his desire as an act of survival.

Her husband and her children occupied spaces at the dinner table in dark, undefined silhouettes, as if they were witnesses whose identities were being masked. She was not shocked by this. It was not that these stolid, regular people she held together with daft toughness and maternal Saran Wrap were anonymous; it was that she was really anonymous to them, and had been for a long time. She held no one to account. It was life. She was, again by the perverse charts of life, not anonymous to the frilly-legged, petty-larcenous, pumpkin-headed, overheated lawn boy. Nor would he be anonymous to her.

Suddenly, it seemed, as if her thinking the child's head resembled a pumpkin two weeks before had precipitated it, Halloween was upon her, and with it distractions she found unnerving. Somehow Halloween had come to epitomize the problems in her life. At the least of it there was what she called the "dick costume frenzy," which meant divining the particular misconceptions three children might have about what fairies and pirates and cats were supposed to look like and then purchasing—at a costume store, mind you—the exotic effects that would satisfy these bizarre whims, and then sewing . . . and it did not end, it seemed, for weeks. Her husband, who might have been counted on to scrooge a minor holiday, instead fanned the flames by entering the children in town costume contests and by volunteering as escort to their candy-gathering caravans. The ban on treats not factory-wrapped was of course de rigueur, but last year someone had rented a metal detector. When Mrs. Hollingsworth saw a set of parents who did not know how to drive their Volvos very well place a bag of candy on a lawn and run a metal detector over it as if it were a bomb, she herself wanted to explode. She wanted to include Halloween in her catalogue of what constituted the South: ". . . stray pets collected and neutered by alcoholics, unless it rains; automotive mechanical intelligence in inverse proportion to dental health; and *Halloween*." She knew that it wasn't the South exclusively that had Tupperwared it: inside the container the middle-class abiders, outside the Candy Man. Inside, afraid to live normal lives, were magazine subscribers running scared; outside, people not reading the news, unless it concerned themselves, not abiding but getting away with things. Her logic loosened at this point to include, rashly, the entire modern world: people fretting in tight well-mannered circles of timid custodial correctness and those circling them with bright eyes. Halloween was as far as you needed to go to see how far along the world was on the road to hell and how big the handcart was.

In this distraction, Mrs. Hollingsworth forgot about the lawn boy until he appeared again on her stoop wearing a suit and a fedora.

"Not another one," she said, referring to costumes.

"No, ma'am," the boy said, removing his hat. "It's me."

"I know it's you," Mrs. Hollingsworth said. "You think I'd have *two* boys stealing lawn mowers for me?"

"I don't know *what* you'd have, lady." He looked her in the eye. This was a fully matured something with a mouth on it, she thought, like a baby snake.

"You *ought* to have me in before they spot me." She swung open the door and swept her arm into the foyer, into which the lawn boy strode, hitching the pants of his too large suit and looking, she thought, for a place to throw the hat. She had a momentary loss of composure as Andy Hardy crossed her mind, and she might have lost her nerve altogether had the child hung the hat on anything. But he did, instead, something rather redeeming: he went directly to the kitchen, opened the sink cabinet, and put the hat, and then the suit, which he removed, revealing the same white shirt and surrey-frilled pants as before, into the trash compactor.

"That's the old man's and that's the old brother's," he said, hitting the compactor switch. "They're dumb. All I knew, they'd have the joint staked out."

Mrs. Hollingsworth started laughing, aware that it might suggest again to the boy that she was laughing at him. But the boy sat at the kitchen table, apparently not bothered by her laughing, and drummed his fingernails. With a short glass of whiskey and some smoke in the room and a little hair on his face he'd have looked a seasoned drinker in a bar.

She got to the table and sat, trying to behave herself, wiping tears from her eyes. "God, I'm sorry."

"For what?"

For what indeed. "Do you steal much?"

"Whenever," he said. He looked around, finally at the calendar on which she recorded family doings: lessons, parties, drudge.

"Have you ever been arrested?"

"You talk a lot, lady," he said, and laughed himself. "I'm kidding."

She looked at him: he was playing a part. He *was* a card.

"It's a strange thing," he said. "You'd never get caught taking a whole lawn mower, for some reason. I got caught once. You know what for?

"What for?"

"Do you know what a WD–40 straw is?"

"No."

"It's a straw . . . a red plastic straw too skinny to even stir coffee or something. It, it sprays WD–40. It costs about nothing. It comes *with* the WD–40, for free. I got caught stealing one. It's six inches long. It's red."

"What's your name, son?"

He looked at her, rather sharply she thought, and she also thought, Not acting now. She said, before she knew why, but immediately knew why, "I mean, what's your name?"

"Jimmy." His attitude said, That's better.

"Jimmy what?"

"Well . . . I thought this would be a, ah, first names only, like a hot line."

"No, it won't."

"Teeth."

"What?"

"My name."

"Your name what?"

"Jimmy Teeth."

"Jimmy Teeth."

"Yes'm." He said this squarely, defiantly.

"Jimmy Teeth," she said, "I'm Janice Halsey," and extended her hand to him. He shook it, firmly.

"You ain't no Mrs. Halsey."

"No, I'm not no *Mrs*. Halsey."

She couldn't tell if he got this, nor could she expect him to know it was not a lie but her maiden name. It seemed time to use her maiden name again with a twelve-year-old suitor, or whatever he was.

"Okay," he said, "Janice Halsey."

"Okay, Jimmy Teeth." She wondered if *he* was lying but didn't think he was. He'd have said Jimmy Diamond if he was lying.

A silence followed which could have been, as Mrs. Hollingsworth's laughing earlier could have been, misinterpreted, caused in this case by the awkwardness of Jimmy Teeth's name or Mrs. Hollingsworth's apparent lying about hers, or both, but it seemed finally just a silence, an odd, agreeable calm between two people in a situation that would presumably not make for agreeable calm. A boy who had stolen lawn mowers and clothes to present, apparently, a boundless need, who had to be no matter how savvy on some levels completely innocent on others, who had in disguise matriculated in the kitchen of a woman whose reactions to his proposition he could not possibly predict, who had to be therefore in part terrified, sat before that random, unknown woman twenty-five years his senior as placid as a gangster; the woman who entertained him, entertained his lunatic hope, who had borne children before another woman had borne this one, who had certain fears of the sexual abuse of children, who had once allowed death-do-us-part vows be read before her as she smiled and cried in an expensive white dress and believed, who had packed lunches and packed the issue of that marriage off to school and that husband off to work, who had had soap-opera days and ironing and long adult afternoons, who had had Sunday brunch and vacations on tropical islands and new station wagons and could read *Bovary* in the French and whose parents were dead, looked calmly at the boy who had stolen a lawn mower and clothes and calmly looked back at her.

She let the moment continue—suspire, as she was wont to put it.

"Well," Jimmy Teeth said, "*do* you like it?"

"Like what?"

"The South."

"Oh. Sure."

"Me too."

He has no idea what he's talking about, she thought. He's making talk. Her job, as superior here, was to rescue him from babbling. He'd shown that under ordinary circumstances he was not prone to babble or to other loose business. But still, the non-awkwardness of the definitively awkward minuet they were in continued to please her.

"The thing about the South," she said, getting up with the sudden perfect idea that she have a drink—a very sweet Manhattan struck her in the cortex, and she got Jimmy Teeth the lemonade the law had earlier cost him—"the thing about the South is that it's a vale of tears that were shed a long time ago. It's a vale of *dry* tears." She looked at Jimmy Teeth.

"Yes'm," he said. "Good ade." He thought that this woman was likely too square for him. She had probably not gotten any further in the video age than, say, Pac-Man and Donkey Kong, if that. She had on some kind of sweater without buttons.

"Do you understand?" she was saying. "A vale of dry tears stands in relation to true weeping as dry cleaning stands to true washing and cleaning."

"Yes'm, I got that."

They sipped their drinks, and Jimmy Teeth feared that the thing had gone this far and yet might not work— how could it do that? Where would he begin anew, with whom? Talk about a vale of dry tears—when Mrs. Hollingsworth again extended her hand to him, only this time it was flat on the table, palm up. The only thing he could figure to do was cover it with his, noting his dirty fingernails and thinking his mother was right in her constant failing fingernail vigilance. Mrs. Hollingsworth

covered his hand with her other one and pressed their
hands together and Jimmy Teeth felt something he had
not yet felt in all the considerable feeling of himself he
had done to date. He felt a surge of something like liquid that came up warmly into his shoulders and head
and almost made him cry.

Mrs. Hollingsworth looked down at the table between her arms, and Jimmy Teeth thought *she* was going
to cry. But she did not. He sat there for what seemed a
very long time, knowing he could not move his hand but
not knowing what else he could or couldn't do. He
thought for the first time, What if someone comes in?
He didn't have a lawn mower and his suit was in the
garbage. Explain *that*. Jimmy Teeth could explain a few
things, but he couldn't explain that. Mrs. Hollingsworth
was, like, *praying* still, and he had time to think how he
might try to explain his presence. My lawn mower's *impounded* and my suit's *compacted*. It was funny if you
said it like that, and he laughed. The laugh was like the
other inappropriate moments they had already shared: it
wasn't inappropriate. They had a little territory here that
was, apparently, unique: nothing was inappropriate.
Jimmy Teeth saw that. Mrs. Hollingsworth saw that, too,
though in an ironic light.

She was not praying. She was thinking. She was
thinking that in this bog of impropriety she was preparing to take Jimmy Teeth and herself into there was only
one truly immoral mire, and that was to act *older* than he
was. She could *be* older, she could be more experienced,
she could take him in ten minutes where he'd take ten
years to get on the streets of sex, and that would be that,
but if she pulled rank, if she mothered him or protected

him or even counseled him, she would be as wrong as the book on this sort of thing said she was. Jimmy Teeth's presumed maturity, the young manliness that dared him into her life with his speaking pumpkin head on a fence and his trembling string-sized legs pushing stolen internal combustion all over her expensively landscaped, highly mortgaged family estate, would be the terra firma for their slouching into a swamp as potentially messy as this one.

"Jimmy," she said, looking him in the eye and despite herself feeling a tenderness for another human being she had not felt in a long time, "Jimmy, I'm going to show you something."

"Yes!" Jimmy Teeth said, making them both laugh.

"Jimmy, first, if I raise you from five dollars to, say, eight, for the lawn, you won't tell Mr. Hollingsworth, will you?"

"That would be a private matter between you and me," Jimmy Teeth said.

"And, Jimmy?"

"Yes'm?"

"Do you go trick or treating?"

"No'm, I quit that."

That was the right answer. Mrs. Hollingsworth made herself another drink. Jimmy was free to pour himself another lemonade if he wanted one. From there on, Jimmy Teeth was on his own. Mrs. Hollingsworth was not on her own, but to the extent she became Janice Halsey again, which was a journey that partook of Orpheus' ascent from the underworld with instructions to not look back, with some comical but not ungratifying sex mixed in, she was on her own, too.

[*Scarliotti*

and the Sinkhole

[In the Pic N' Save Green Room, grits were free. Scarliotti, as he liked to call himself, though his real name was Rod, Scarliotti ate free grits in the Green Room. To Rod, grits were virtually sacramental; to Scarliotti they were a joke, and if he could not eat them for free in a crummy joint so down in the world it had to use free grits as a promotional gimmick, he wouldn't eat them. Scarliotti had learned that when he was Rod, treating grits as good food, *he* had been a joke, so he became Scarliotti. He wanted his other new name, his new given name, to come from the province of martial arts. Numchuks Scarliotti was strong but a little obvious. He was looking for something more refined, a name that would not start a fight but would prevent one from starting. He also thought a name from the emergency room might do: Triage Scarliotti, maybe. But he had to be careful there. Not many people knew what terms in the emergency room meant. Suture Scarliotti, maybe. Edema Scarliotti. Lavage Scarliotti. No, he liked the martial-arts idea better. With his new name he would be a new man, one who would never eat grits with a straight face again.

There were many things he never intended to do with a straight face again. One of them was ride Tomos, a Yugoslavian moped that would go about twenty miles per hour flat out, and get clipped in the head by a mirror on a truck pulling a horse trailer and wake up with a head wound with horseshit in it in the hospital. Another was to be grateful that at least Tomos had not been hurt. Now, his collection of a quarter million dollars in damages imminent, he didn't give a shit about a motorized bicycle. He wasn't riding that and he wasn't seriously eating grits anymore. He was going to take a cab the rest of his life and eat grits only if they were free. He would never again be on the side of the road and never pay for grits, and it might just be *Mister* Scarliotti. Deal with that.

The horse Yankees who clipped him were in a world of hurt and he wanted them to be. They were the kind of yahoos who leave Ohio and find a tract of land that was orange groves until 1985 and now is plowed out and called a horse farm and buy it and fence it and call themselves horse breeders. And somehow they breed Arabian horses, and somehow it is Arabs behind it all. Somehow Minute Maid, which is really Coca-Cola, leaves, and Kuwait and Ohio are here. And the Yankees are joking and laughing about grits at first, and then they wise up and try to fit in and start eating them every morning after learning how to cook them, which it takes them about a year to do it. And driving all over the state in diesel doolies with mirrors coming off them about as long as airplane wings, and knocking *people who live here* in the ditch.

Scarliotti is in his motorized bed in his trailer in Hague, Florida. It is only ten o'clock but the trailer is already ticking in the heat. Scarliotti swears it—the trailer—moves, kind of bends, on its own, when he is lying still in the bed, and not even moving the bed, which has an up for your head and an up for your feet and both together kind of make a sandwich out of you; hard to see the TV that way, which is on an arm just like at the hospital and controlled by a remote just like at the hospital, a remote on a thick white cord, which he doesn't understand why it isn't like a remote everybody else has at their house. When the trailer moves, Scarliotti thinks that a sinkhole might be opening up. Before his accident that would have been fine. But not now. Two hundred and fifty thousand dollars would be left topside if he went down a sinkhole today, and even if he *lived* down there, which he thought was possible, he knew he couldn't spend *that* kind of money down there. He thought about maybe asking Higgins, whom he worked for before the accident, if they could put outriggers or something on the trailer to keep it from going down. They could cable it to the big oak, but the big oak might go itself. He didn't know. He didn't know if outriggers would work or not. A trailer wasn't a canoe, and the dirt was not water.

There were about a hundred pills on a tray next to him he was supposed to take but he hadn't been, and now they were piled up and he had started throwing them out the back window and he hoped they didn't *grow* or something and give him away. You could get busted for anything these days. It was not like the old days.

Tomos was beside the trailer, and Scarliotti had asked his daddy to get it running, and if his daddy had, he could get to the Lil' Champ for some beer before the nurse came by. The bandages and the bald side of his head scared the clerk at the Lil' Champ, and once she undercharged him, she was so scared. He let that go, but he didn't like having done it because he liked her and she'd have to pay for it. But right now he couldn't afford to correct an error in his favor. Any day now, he'd be able to afford to correct all the errors in his favor in the world. He was going to walk in the Lil' Champ and buy the entire glass beer cooler, so he might as well buy the whole store and the girl with it. See how scared she got then.

He accidentally hit both buttons on the bed thing and squeezed himself into a sandwich and it made him pee in his pants before he could get it down, but he did not care. It didn't matter now if you peed in your pants in your bed. It did not matter now.

—

He tried to start Tomos by push-starting it, and by the time he gave up he was several hundred yards from the trailer. It was too far to walk it back and he couldn't leave it where it was so he pushed Tomos with him to the Lil' Champ. He had done this before. The girl watched him push the dead moped up and lean it against the front of the store near the paper racks and the doors so he could keep a eye on it.

Scarliotti did not greet her but veered to the cooler and got a twelve-pack of Old Mil and presented it at the counter and began digging for his money. It had gotten in his left pocket again, which was a bitch because he had to get it out with his right hand because his left couldn't since the accident. Crossing his body this way and pronating his arm to dig into his pocket threw him into a bent slumped contortion.

The girl chewed gum fast to keep from laughing at Scarliotti. She couldn't help it. Then she got a repulsive idea, but she was bored so she went ahead with it.

"Can I help you?" she asked.

Scarliotti continued to wrestle with himself, looking like a horror-movie hunchback to her. His contorting put the wounded part of his head just above the countertop between them. It was all dirty hair and scar and Formica and his grunting. She came from behind the counter and put one hand on Scarliotti's little back and pulled his twisted hand out of his pocket and slipped hers in. Scarliotti froze. She held her breath and looked at his poor forlorn moped leaning against the brick outside and hoped she could get the money without touching anything else.

Scarliotti braced his two arms on the counter and held still and then suddenly stuck his butt out into her and made a noise and she felt, as she hoped she wouldn't, a hardening the size of one of those small purple bananas they don't sell in the store but are very good, Mexicans and people eat them. She jerked her hand out with a ten-dollar bill in it.

Scarliotti put his head down on the counter and began taking deep breaths.

"Do you want to go on a date?" he asked her, his head still down as if he were weeping.

"No." She rang up the beer.

"Any day now I will be pert a millionaire."

"Good."

"Good? *Good? Shit.* A *mil*lionaire."

She started chewing rapidly again. "Go ahead and be one," she said.

"You don't believe me?"

"You going be Arnold Schwarzenegger, too?"

This stopped Scarliotti. It was a direction he didn't understand. He made a guess. "*What?* You don't think I'm strong?" Before the girl could answer, he ran over to the copy machine and picked up a corner of it and would have turned it over but it started to roll and got away and hit the magazine rack. Suddenly, inexplicably, he was sad. He did not do sad. Sad was bullshit.

"Don't think I came," he said to the girl.

"What?"

"I didn't *come.* That's *pee!*" He left the store with dignity and pushed Tomos with the beer strapped to the little luggage rack over the rear wheel to the trailer and did not look back at approaching traffic. Hit him *again,* for all he cared.

In the trailer there wasn't shit on the TV, people in costumes he couldn't tell what they were, screaming Come on down! or something. He put the beer in the freezer. He sat against the refrigerator feeling the trailer tick and bend. Shit like that wouldn't happen if his daddy would fix damn Tomos. His daddy was letting him down. He was—he had an idea something like he was letting himself down. This was preposterous. How did one do, or not do, that? Do you extend outriggers from yourself? Can a canoe in high water just grow its own outriggers? No, it can't.

A canoe in high water takes it or it goes down. End of chapter. He drank a beer and popped a handful of the pills for the nurse and knew that things were not going to change. This was it. It was foolish to believe in anything but a steady continuation of things exactly as they are at this moment. This moment was it. This was it. Shut the fuck *up*.

He was dizzy. The trailer ticked in the sun and he felt it bending and he felt himself also ticking in some kind of heat and bending. He was dizzy, agreeably. It did not feel bad. The sinkhole that he envisioned was agreeable, too. He hoped that when the trailer went down it went smoothly, like a glycerine suppository. No protest, no screaming, twisting, scraping. The sinkhole was the kind of thing he realized that other people had when they had Jesus. He didn't need Jesus. He had a *hole*, and it was a purer thing than a *man*.

—

He was imagining life in the hole—how cool? how dark? how wet? Bats or blind catfish? The most positive speculation he could come up with was it was going to save on air conditioning, then maybe on clothes. Maybe you could walk around naked, and what about all the things that had gone down sinkholes over the years, *houses* and shit, at your disposal maybe—he heard a noise and thought it was the nurse and jumped in bed and tried to look asleep, but when the door opened and someone came in he knew it wasn't the nurse and opened his eyes. It was his father.

"Daddy," he said.

"Son."

"You came for Tomos?"

"I'mone Tomos your butt."

"What for?" Rather than have to hear the answer, which was predictable even though he couldn't guess what it would be, Scarliotti wished he had some of those sharp star things you throw in martial arts to pin his daddy to the trailer wall and get things even before this started happening. His father was looking in the refrigerator and slammed it. He had not found the beer. If you didn't drink beer you were too stupid to know where people who do drink it keep it after a thirty-minute walk in Florida in July. Scarliotti marveled at this simple luck of his.

He looked up and saw his daddy standing too close to him, still looking for something.

"The doctor tells me you ain't following directions."

"What directions?"

"*All* directions."

Scarliotti wasn't following any directions but didn't know how anybody knew.

"You got to be *hungry* to eat as many pills as they give me."

"You got to be *sober* to eat them pills, son."

"That, too."

The headboard above Scarliotti's head rang with a loudness that made Scarliotti jerk and made his head hurt, and he thought he might have peed some more. His father had backhanded the headboard.

"If we'd ever get the money," Scarliotti said, "but that lawyer you picked I don't think knows shit—"

"He knows plenty of shit. It ain't his fault."

"It ain't my fault."

"No, not beyond getting hit by a truck."

"Oh. That's *my* fault."

"About."

Scarliotti turned on the TV and saw Adam yelling something at Dixie. Maybe it was Adam's crazy brother. This was the best way to get his father to leave. "Shhh," he said. "This is my show." Dixie had a strange accent. "Don't fix it, then."

"Fix what?" his father said.

"Tomos."

"Forget that damned thing."

"I can't," Scarliotti said to his father, looking straight at him. "I love her."

His father stood there a minute and then left. Scarliotti peeked through the curtains and saw that he was again not taking the bike to get it fixed for him.

He got a beer and put the others in the refrigerator just in time. He wanted sometimes to have a beer joint and *really* sell the coldest beer in town, not just say it. He heard another noise outside and jumped back in bed with his beer. Someone knocked on the door. That wouldn't be his father. He put the beer under the covers.

"Come in."

It was the nurse.

"Come in, *Ma*ma," Scarliotti said when he saw her.

"Afternoon, Rod."

He winced but let it go. They thought in the medical profession you had mental problems if you changed your name. They didn't know shit about mental problems, but it was no use fighting them so he let them call him Rod.

The nurse was standing beside the bed looking at the pill tray, going "Tch, tch, tch."

"I took a bunch of 'em," Scarliotti said.

The nurse was squinching her nose as if she smelled something.

"I know you want to get well, Rod," she said.

"I am well," he said.

"Not by a long shot," she said.

"I ain't going *to the moon*," he said.

The nurse looked curiously at him. "No," she said, "you're not."

Scarliotti thought he had put her in her place. He liked her but didn't like her preaching crap at him. He was well enough to spend the $250,000, and that was as well as he needed to be. It was the Yankee Arab horse breeders were sick, not well enough to pay their debts when they go running over people because they're retired and don't have shit else to do. The nurse was putting the arm pump-up thing on his arm. She had slid some of the pills around with her weird little pill knife that looked like a sandwich spreader or something. He wanted to show her his Buck knife, but would reveal the beer and the pee if he got it out of his pocket.

"It's high, again. If you have another fit, you're back in the hospital."

"I'm not having no nother fit."

Scarliotti looked at her chest. The uniform was white and ribbed, and made a starchy little tissuey noise when she moved, and excited him. He looked closely at the ribs in the material when she got near him.

"Them lines on your shirt look like . . . crab lungs," he said.

"What?"

"I don't know, like crab lungs. You know what I mean?"

"No, Rod, I don't." She rolled her eyes and he saw her. She shouldn't do that. That was what he meant when he said, and he was right, that the medical profession did not know shit about mental problems.

The nurse went over everything again, two this four that umpteen times ninety-eleven a day, which meant you'd be up at two and three and five in the morning taking pills if you bought the program, and left. He watched Barney Fife get his bullet taken back by Andy. He wanted to see Barney *keep* his bullet. Barney should be able to keep that bullet. But if Barney shot at his own foot like that, he could see it. Barney was a dumb fuck. Barney looked like he'd stayed up all night taking pills. There was another noise outside. Scarliotti had had it with people fucking with him. He listened. There was a timid knock at the door. He just lay there. Let them break in, he thought. Then, head wound or not, he would kill them.

The door opened and someone called Hello. Then: "Anyone home?"

Scarliotti waited and was not going to say anything

and go ahead and lure them in and kill them, but it was a girl's voice and familiar somehow, but not the nurse, so he said, "If you can call it that."

The girl from the Lil' Champ stepped in.

"I'm down here."

She looked down the hall and saw him and came down it with a package.

"You paid for a case," she said.

"I could use a case," Scarliotti said.

"Pshew," the girl said. Even so, she was, it seemed, being mighty friendly.

"Well, let's have us one," Scarliotti said.

The girl got two beers out of the package.

"You like Andy Griffin?" he said.

"*Fith*. He's okay. Barney's funny. Floyd is creepy."

"Floyd?"

"Barber? In the chair?"

"Oh." Scarliotti had no idea what she was talking about. Goober and Gomer, he knew. The show was over anyway. He turned the set off, holding up the white remote rig to show the girl.

"They let you off to deliver that beer?"

"I'm off."

"Oh."

"On my way."

"Oh."

Scarliotti decided to go for it. "I would dog to dog you." He blushed, so he looked directly at her to cover for it, with his eyes widened.

"That's about the nastiest idea I ever heard," the girl said.

"My daddy come by here a while ago, took a *swang* at me," Scarliotti said. "Then the nurse come by and give me a raft of shit. I nearly froze the beer. Been a rough day."

"You would like to make love to me. Is that what you're saying?" Since she had touched him in the store and he had said what he said, the girl had undergone a radical change of heart about Scarliotti's repulsiveness. She did not understand it, exactly.

Scarliotti had never in his life heard anyone say, "You would like to make love to me," nor had he said it to anyone, and did not think he could, even if it meant losing a piece of ass. He stuck by his guns.

"I would dog to dog you."

"Okay."

The girl stood up and took her clothes off. Compared to magazines she was too white and puffy, but she was a girl and she was already getting in the bed. For a minute Scarliotti thought they were fighting and then it was all warm and solid and they weren't. He said "Goddamn" several times. "God*damn*." He looked at the headboard and saw what looked like a dent where his father had backhanded it and was wondering if he was wearing a ring done that or just hit it that fucking hard with his hand when the girl bit his neck. "Ow!" he said. "*Goddamn.*"

"You fucker," the girl said.

"Okay," Scarliotti said, trying to be agreeable.

"*Good*," she said.

Then it was over and she no longer looked too white and soft. She was sweaty and red. Some of Scarliotti's hair had fallen out on her from the good side of his head and he hoped nothing had fallen out of the bad side. The trailer had stopped moving from their exertions. There were ten beers sweating onto a hundred pills beside the bed. The nurse and his father would not be back before the trailer could start ticking in the heat and bending on its own, unless they bent it again themselves with exertions in the bed, but all in all Scarliotti thought it would be a good enough time to have some fun without being bothered by anyone before the trailer found its way down the hole.

———

Scarliotti woke up and took the sweating beers in his arms and put them in the refrigerator and came back with two cold ones. "They *look* like a commercial sitting there but they don't *taste* like a commercial," he said, waking and mystifying the girl. "Women," he said, feeling suddenly very good about things, "know what they want and how to get it. Men are big fucking babies."

"How do you come to know all that?" the girl asked.

"I know."

"How many women you had?"

"Counting you?"

"Yeah."

"Three."

"That explains how you know so much."

Scarliotti started laughing. "Heh, heh, heh . . . *heah, heahh, heahhh*—" and did not stop until he was coughing and slumped against the wall opposite the bed.

"Quailhead," he said.

"What?"

"Nothing."

"You call me quailhead?"

"No. You want to go down to the Green Room and eat free grits?"

"Eat free grits," she said flatly, with a note of suspicion.

"Yeah."

"I thought you were going be a millionaire."

"I am. Pert near. That's why I don't pay for grits."

"Well, I still pay for grits. I ain't eating no free grits."

"See? Heh, heh . . . it proves what I said. Women know what they want."

"And men are babies."

Scarliotti started the laugh again and crawled into bed with the girl.

"Be still. Shhh!"

"What?" the girl asked.

"Listen to the trailer."

"I don't hear anything—"

"Listen! Hear that?"

"No."

"It's ticking. It's moving. You ever thought of living in a sinkhole?"

"No."

"You want to go down into a sinkhole with me?"

"No."

"You want to go to the Hank show?"

"Okay."

"I mean, us all, whole thing going. Trailer and all."

"To the Hank show?"

"No, into the *sinkhole*."

Scarliotti started the uncontrollable heaving laugh

again at this, and the girl reluctantly stroked the shaved side of his head to calm him. At first she barely touched it, but she began to like the moist bristly feel of Scarliotti's wounded head.

—

Scarliotti woke up and looked out the window and saw a dog and a turtle. The dog appeared to be licking the turtle.

"Ballhoggey wollock dube city, man. Your dog," he said to the girl, "is licking that turtle in its *face*. That turtle can *bite*, man. You better get your dog away from that turtle, man. That dog is, unnaturally *friendly*, man. I don't want to even *go* into salmonella. That turtle can kill your dog from here to Sunday. It dudn' *have* to bite him, man. I *don't* want that turtle to bite your dog, man. On the *tongue* like that. I think I'd start, like, crying. I'd cry like a son of a bitch if we had to get that turtle off your dog's tongue. Your dog's tongue would look like a . . . shoe tongue. It would be blue and red. Your dog would be hollering and tears coming out of *its* eyes. That turtle would be squinting and biting down *hard*, man. I don't want it. I don't.

"You better get your dog, man. We'd have to kill that turtle to get it off. If it didn' cut your dog's tongue off first, man. Shit. Take a bite out of it like cheese. This round scallop space, like. God. *Get your dog*, man. I have an appointment somewhere. What time is it? I think this damn Fruit of the Loom underwear is for shit. You see this guy walking around in his underwear with his kid, going to pee, and then popping out this fresh pair of miniature BVD's for the kid just like his, and they walk down the hall real slow in the same stupid tight pants look like *panties*? *Get* your dog, man.

"Shit. Fucking turtle. What's it *doing* here, man? I mean, your *dog's* not even supposed— What time is it? *Get* the bastard, will you? I can't move my . . . legs. I don't know when it happened. Last twenty minutes after I dogged you. I'd get him myself. That dog is . . . not trained or what? Did you train him? People shouldn't let their dogs go anarchy, man. Dogs need government. Dogs are senators in their hearts when they're trained. They have, like white hair and deep voices. And do *right*. Your dog is going to get *bit*, man. Get your dog. Please get your dog. This position I'm in, I don't know how I got in it. It dudn' make sense.

"Do you ever think about J.E.B. Stuart? His name wasn't Jeb, it's initials of J. E. B. He had a orange feather in a white hat and was, like, good. Won. Fast, smart, all that, took no survivors; well, I don't know about that. Kind of kind you want on *your* side, like that. Man. It's hard to talk, say things right. If you don't get your dog I'm going to shoot—you. No, myself. *Claim* your dog out there. The window is dirty as shit. I pay a lot of money for this trailer, you think they'd wash the goddamn window. No, you wouldn't. You *know* they wouldn't wash the goddamn window. I'd shoot the *turtle*, but the window, they wouldn't *fix* it so they wouldn't *wash* it, would they? I'd shoot your fucking *dog* before I'd shoot the turtle. That turtle idn' doing shit but getting licked in the face and *taking* it."

The girl said, "I don't have a dog."

"Well, somebody does," Scarliotti said. "*Some*body sure as hell does."

[*Wayne*

[**W**ayne this morning begins unpacking a box of clay tiles for the HoJo roof in Scottsdale, Arizona, he's supposed to repair. The first seven tiles are broken and that is enough. He is last seen leaving the convenience store across the street with a twelve-pack under his arm, getting nimbly into his car. The carton of tiles is left open, its four top flaps at angles suggesting a funnel.

Wayne's car leaves a fine invisible trail of rust very near the color of the clay tiles. A bloodhound trained in Detroit could track the car, a 1968 Impala. A crime team could locate hairs matching Wayne's along the trail of rust, blond and about seven inches long and not clean. Dental records, were Wayne found in demise, would be of little use identifying him owing to the extremely rapid rate of deterioration—equivalent to dentonic melt-down—of Wayne's mouth. Wayne looks as if he has driven into a swarm of flies as he flies down the highway smiling and drinking and tossing his hair and tossing cans in the desert and forgetting roof tiles and roofs and

HoJos, except for renting a room in one with a blonde, but he saw no blondes when he looked around after opening the carton of broken tiles to see if anyone was sympathetic and saw instead the convenience store and that was enough. Wayne is Wayne and Wayne is gone. *Stone.*

Wayne, in a mirror of his motel room, the name of which he does not know (the motel), the room number of which he'd have to find the key to know, or open and look at the door, too bright a thing to do, Wayne looks at his teeth. He wishes they were like Legos. He could snap them out and snap in new ones, snugly into tight, clean holes, white and firm and solid. The holes in these he has are black with green or yellow edges and not clean, firm, tight holes like in Legos, which hold the Legos together snap-like. These teeth are rotten to hell. How they got this way is about how his liver got its way: a thing that mysteriously, suddenly, but not really, hurts. The teeth, the mirror, his right side, changing all the fun things he likes to do or he'll die is a shame. "It's a shame," he almost says, looking at his teeth and thinking of a cold beer, but he doesn't say "It's a shame," he laughs and looks in the cooler at the foot of the bed for that beer. And *it's there*. He is, after all, the most lucky of men, at 10:30 in the morning in the Arizona desert. The bed, he notices, is not even disturbed; he slept on top of it, like a big cat. The maid will only have to plump it and tuck it a bit. He did not get his money's worth here. But he has a cold Coors and the motel management isn't Pakistani, so he's not going to get under the covers now just to mess the bed up. He's going to get in his car and get some cigarettes and chips and more beer and drive into the worthless future and enjoy the shit out of it.

The white thighs of his wife, who was not really ugly, white like Boy-ar-dee noodles, which he really got off on, occur to him and give him a little momentary woody. That's what cigarettes and more beer are good against, errant and unfair woodies at 10:30 in the morning. Woodies out of the blue with no help in sight. He could wait for the maid . . . *right*. He could instead fire up the Impala, 357 *loud* cubic inches, and get the goddamn beer. That is the manly, sane thing to do. Felicia *was* ugly. So is the desert.

It doesn't have any *trees*. This cactus shit and mesquite shit is shit. Felicia was shit-for-brains and the desert is shit-for-trees. It does not look like rain—what else is new, in the desert. It doesn't look like anything, in the desert. When things don't look like anything, drive through them. And don't try it alone: have help. Have Coors, Winstons, Doritos, cardboard coasters placed under your icy mug by a woman in tight polyester shorts at happy hour, a woman who will say "Sure, sugar" when you ask for jukebox change. Apropos of her shorts, you will say, looking now no lower than her forehead, "I'm from Texas." "That right?" "I haven't seen a tree in a month." It's not going well. What else is new. Play the jukebox and don't play what you think she'd like. Play what you like, but you won't know anything on it, so play whatever the hell you want to. You are a free man. Play what you *don't like*, if you like. Go back to the bar and get her to fill your mug, or get her to give you a new icy mug, and say, "I played stuff I don't know if I like it.

They, you know, they have different songs as far as areas." She takes your money, smiling. "What else is new in the desert," you say to her butt, and she says "What?" stopping and looking at you from the register. "Nothing."

There was a girl he met in the Navy in the Philippines. She looked entirely American but swore, in perfect English, which made it harder to believe, that she was Amerasian, a soldier's bastard. When they fucked she started shaking and kept shaking until he thought the cot would come apart. When they were done she put her face in his neck and held it there for a long time, which made him think she was crying and *was* entirely American. Wayne thinks of this now, looking at the woman behind the bar smoking, looking in virtually any direction but his, who calls him "sugar" when making change. The Navy was a desert but it wasn't like this.

"Have you ever heard of a song," Wayne says to the woman behind the bar, "called 'The Navy Is a Desert but Nothing Like This'?"

"No," she says.

"Good song."

"I bet, sugar."

"No, you don't," Wayne says under his breath.

"You ready?"

"No," he says, and walks out, anticipating the secure barreling unfraught ease of the heavy Impala on straight road. He hopes for a no-Pakistani motel tonight, but even on that he's wearing down. "No Pakistani ever called me redneck," he says to the rearview mirror, laughing. This gives him the cheering idea of registering in Pakistani motels as Muhammad Ali. That would establish everyone on even footing, somehow. "Mr. Ali will need a bar of soap," he will tell them. "Mr. Ali will need sheets that are white." "Mr. Ali will thank Allah for whiteness and soap." He's lost his mind and he doesn't mind. He hates bathing. There's not a Pakistani in the world dirtier than he is. Some guys in the Navy once had to gang-wash him. But still. White is white.

—

Wayne goes home. California was out. There was, all in all, too much desert between his hangover leave-takings of Pakistani motels and his not altogether enticing visions of California. These were of Beverly Hillsesque inaccessibility and of Venice Beach, where everyone, including the women, had more muscles than Wayne did. All he could see was pink skates and purple spandex and no pussy at one end of things, and movie-star houses seen through a bus window on the other. So he turned around. There was nothing to go home to, but there was nothing to not go home to. He wondered if driving back over the same ground would have the effect of making the desert look different, possibly better (it couldn't get worse). The phenomenon he had in mind was of how carpet sometimes looked different if you looked at it from the other side of the room. He wondered if the desert was like that. He bought five cases of Coors and did not plan to stop at any more motels, Pakistani or not. When he had packed the beer strategically in the trunk and got back in the Impala—he thought of the beer as ammo for a protracted military campaign—there was a bird in it with him. "Stone!" he said to the bird, fired up the car, and planned to have the bird cross the desert backwards with him. About a mile down the road the bird lit on his shoulder, shat on his shirtfront, and flew out the driver's window in front of Wayne's face.

That was the desert for you. In the Philippines birds sat around on their own perches and talked to you. How a God-made, natural thing like the desert that was so *Santa Fe* and all that and Indian holy shit ground and Hopi boogie shit got to be worse off than a man-made piece of shit like the Navy and Subic Bay and two-dollar blow jobs from skinny guys' little sisters was beyond Wayne.

[**W**hen Wayne got back from not going to California, the HoJo in Scottsdale still leaking, he hoped, but didn't see how, since if it rained in the desert it wouldn't be much, he drove over to his and Felicia's house, which was now Felicia's and the kids', and walked in as if it were still his, too. Felicia was standing on what looked like a miniature walker for old folks. It had four chrome legs about a foot high and a pink vinyl pad on the top and was slanted backwards just like a walker. Only, Felicia was standing on it and looking at herself in the mirror over the sofa. Wayne reached under the cushions of the sofa and withdrew his Army WWI bayonet, which he had kept against intruders when he lived there.

"What the hell you doing?" he asked Felicia.

"This," Felicia said, turning one way and another to look at her hips, which were in pink shorts the exact color of the vinyl pad she stood on, "is a Exerstep."

"A what?"

"You step on it."

"I see that. Any beer?"

"No."

Wayne looked at his bayonet: it was the narrow kind, very heavy, with the most prodigious blood groove he had ever seen on a knife of any kind. It was not imaginable to him that a bayonet like this one could kill someone better, or more efficiently or quickly, or let you get it out of the victim easier, or whatever the hell a blood groove actually did or was supposed to do. *Blood groove.* It sounded like a joke, or something to tell a recruit and laugh at him if he believed it. It was probably a way to save steel.

Felicia stepped off the Exerstep and back up, and stepped back off and back on, and looked at her hips some more. Wayne pressed his crotch to her leg, at about her knee.

"Hey, ugly."

"Don't say that to me, Wayne."

"Okay. How about a knobber?"

"Not now. Later."

"Sounds like a weenie."

Wayne struck an elaborate, stylized martial-arts pose and said, "I'm a burnin, burnin hunk of love," and threw the bayonet at the back of the front door, which it struck not with the blade but with the short, heavy, fat machined handle, making a deep, dull contusion in the door and falling to the floor with a thick twang. Two boys ran into the room at the sound and saw immediately the bayonet and the fresh wound in the door and Wayne and said, in unison and looking at Felicia to gauge her approval, *"Cool!"* Felicia was expressionless, so the boys leaped on the bayonet and fought over it until Wayne took it from them and put it through his belt pirate-style.

"Git."

The boys did.

"There *is* some beer, I think, Wayne," Felicia said.

"Who brought it?"

"Nobody."

"Nobody, shit."

"Nobody, Wayne."

"*I* didn't leave it."

"Wayne, *you left*."

"Okay. Okay. Don't give me the fifth amendment or third-degree burns or—" He stopped speaking, overcome by the sight of Felicia's pale thigh going into the Exerstep-pink nylon so loosely a hand could easily glide up there, meeting no restriction.

"Our Lady of Prompt Succor!" he declared, brandishing the bayonet and trying to kiss her.

"Don't. I'm sweaty."

"Okay."

Felicia went to shower and Wayne went to the kitchen, where he parted items in the refrigerator with the bayonet until he found the beer. These he would have stabbed to extract if it wouldn't have wasted a beer. He felt good, suddenly very good. He almost took a beer into the back yard and punctured it with the bayonet to test out the blood groove, but did not. Yet. "Goddamn *beer groove*," he said aloud, holding a beer in one hand and the bayonet in the other. He regarded the bayonet and its groove a moment, put it on top of the refrigerator, and walked back into the living room holding his crotch, with certain fingers extended and certain folded as he'd seen black rappers do. The fingering was the same as the Texas Longhorn Hook 'em Horns sign.

—

What do they call it—fragrant dereliction?
What?
Romans. Somebody. Napoleons.
Be quiet.
I'm about to pop.
Don't.
I could come back, do this to you all the time.
No, you couldn't!
Come back, do it sometimes.
Not come back. Sometimes, maybe.
Whatever. *Changkaichek*!
Oh, Wayne.
Hey. That mudpuppy'll be back hard in ten minutes.
I don't have ten minutes.
What?
Work.
Sounds like a personal problem.
Actually, it *is*, Wayne. I have to have two jobs now.
Oh.
And . . .
And what?
Don't be here when I get back, if you want *sometimes*.
Shee*yit*.
That's right.

—

Wayne left without showering, wondering where Felicia's second job was, where she . . . how she took care of four kids. It was a vague, troubling haze of guilt that felt like a huge ball of tangled monofilament filling the back seat of the car. A ball of monofilament that size could not be dealt with with less than a flamethrower. It would ensnare birds, it would hook something, it would trip you, you'd see a piece of good tackle in it and never cut your way in, it would foul your next cast, it would williefy your entire life. If his life was a happy, larky fishing trip, he had a ball of monofilament half the size of the boat beside him. And it didn't have anything to do with him anymore. Felicia had had it. She wouldn't *let* him untangle it. Which he didn't want to, couldn't do anyway. How did marriage and kids look like such a hot idea before you had it and like such a clusterfuck after you got it? It was like praying for rain and getting struck by lightning.

"I feel like going to Italy," Wayne said aloud in the Impala. He pictured wearing rather pointy, thin-soled shoes and yelling at people without having to fight them and drinking things he'd never heard of (and *liking* them) and mountains, maybe, and fountains and marble and beautiful women who would talk to you whether you understood them or not and whether they understood you or not, a problem that sign language would solve anyway, and what it would be like sleeping with dark world-famous-loving women who did not wear pink shorts the same pink as a miniature geezer walker, stepping on it about once an hour. He was ready for a beer. He was not ready for the want ads, but it looked like time.

[**W**ayne drove down to a bar called Taco Flats run by an agreeable Mexican who would pretend he understood your bad Spanish. Blocking the lot to Taco Flats were cars lined up to do window banking at the bank next door. Wayne wished one of them would just rob the bank and dismiss the line of traffic. He wondered why he didn't rob the bank. He had the bayonet, against the day Felicia cut him off and changed the locks and denied him his things, or moved in the night with them all, or whatever a woman going up and down on a geezer walker might come up with. He could rob the bank with his bad Spanish and a bayonet. *"Cabrónes! Tú probablamente anticipare un hombre* with *pistole. Es un blood groove!" Blood groove* shouted by a white-looking Mexican bandito would scare anyone in a bank in suburban San Antonio. The line of cars opened for him and he drove into the Taco Flats lot. It was lunatic to rob a bank without a gun. He had over a hundred dollars left from not going to California, anyway.

The agreeable Mexican who ran Taco Flats, Harry, gave Wayne, whom he had once overlooked passed out at a corner booth and locked in Taco Flats for the night, a wink and said, *"Qué pasa!"*

"Stone!" Wayne said. *"Mongo firo bira, per favor."* He meant to say *frío* beer—cold, a word he knew—but never got it right. This was the sort of error Harry allowed by never correcting. He would in fact corroborate and advance these idiocies people came up with.

"Aquí, a fiery beer, my friend John Wayne."

"Wayne," Wayne said.

"Sí. John Wayne, if you go to sleep and something today, let please a bandanna on the table for indication of surrender."

This was the height of Wayne and Harry's communion: a manly, head-on reference to Wayne's humiliating overnight stay and Harry's jovial acceptance of it.

"Chingasa!" Wayne said, squinting with mirth and a mouthful of extremely cold fiery beer.

Harry would move on to other customers, forgetting Wayne except to ponder how someone as unlike John Wayne got to be called John Wayne. Wayne had no idea how he came to be called, by Harry, John Wayne, but it was in the fabric of not correcting anyone or anything to let it go. Besides, he had tried and it didn't work. He *drank* like John Wayne, Wayne thought, if John Wayne drank. Did John Wayne drink? Did Dean Martin say, "Circle the wagons, the Injuns are comin'"? Were dress designers gay? These models you saw, runway, were so goddamned *good-looking*. He tried to picture Calvin Klein or Perry Ellis in the Navy. He couldn't. He could see male models in Klein underwear in the Navy but not Calvin Klein himself. He did not have the *balls* to rob a bank. Bayonet, Biretta, shit, *Uzi*. Kalashnikov. He wouldn't rob a bank with a bazooka. He wouldn't hold up Fort Knox with an atom bomb. He couldn't do shit.

Well, why *should* he? What was wrong, exactly, with not having the balls to rob a bank? Someone tell him that. Someone tell him what was wrong with being afraid to rob a bank. He wished he had had it out with that woman in the desert who called him Sugar. It wouldn't have worked. "You've never heard the song 'The Navy Is a Desert but Nothing Like This'? Do you think it's unmanly of me not to rob a bank? Do you?" She would have said no. And that would have been the end of it. It was hard to get anyone to actually talk to you, and harder, if they did, to get them to make sense.

In this reverie Wayne suddenly smelled tar pitch. He looked around. People had come in. A black guy was saying to Harry, "Harry, is *Cabriolet* a goat and a Chevrolet or what?" Harry looked at him. "You know, man," the black guy said, *"cabrito."* The guy had on a T-shirt with a picture of the Last Supper or something on it over the words IT'S A BLACK THING. YOU WOULDN'T UNDERSTAND. Wayne thought the wearer of the shirt ought to understand what the fuck a Cabriolet was. It was a goddamned car.

"It's a *car*, Stone," Wayne said loudly. He had the balls to do that. The black guy looked at him and Wayne realized the tar-pitch smell was coming from him. "You a hot man, Stone?"

The black guy turned back to the bar and ignored him.

Wayne went up to within two stools of him. He could see the left side of the table of black luminaries on the guy's shirt. The figure closest to him looked like Jesse Jackson. That seemed right to Wayne: he'd never understood Jesse Jackson. You'd think anyone who spoke in rhymes to uneducated people in the ghetto would be understandable, but he was not, to Wayne. Wayne called Harry and bought the black guy a beer and had Harry give it to him, and when the black guy looked at him Wayne said, more embarrassed than he anticipated being, "I don't understand Jesse Jackson," and the black guy looked at him as if he was crazy.

"Well," Wayne said, apologizing by raising his palms off the bar in a shrug, "I don't. I just don't. *Cocaine* is a *pain* in yo' *brain*, I guess I get that. No, I don't even get that. It feels pretty good to mine. You work hot roofing, right?"

"Okay," the black guy said.

This threw Wayne a bit. *Okay?* Okay *what*?

"Okay what?" Wayne said.

"The beer."

"Oh. Okay."

Wayne drank his own beer as a kind of confirmation that they were drinking together. That seemed to be the way the black guy took it, too. When they had finished the beers the black guy bought the round and Harry gave Wayne a beer without having to acknowledge where it came from. Wayne said "Stoweno" to Harry.

To the black guy he said, "I work cold."

"Cold?"

"Cold process."

"What that?"

"No kettle. Shit in cans, barrels."

"Sticky shit."

"Yeah."

"Man. No."

"Better'n burning your ass."

"Stick your ass to everything."

"*Más o meno*."

"You don't understand Jesse Jackson?"

"No."

"*I* don't understand Mickey Mantle."

"Sounds like a wiener."

"What?"

"I dig it."

"You crazy."

"Stoweno."

Wayne was smiling at all this and the black guy was shaking his head, not altogether unamused. Wayne had no idea what the black guy was talking about or why he was smiling. He looked about 230, most of it in his shoulders. The black guy had had some pot after work and the two beers, and he was feeling frisky because Wayne looked about 90 pounds wet and the bartender was a largish Mexican, not a small one.

"What I want to know," the black guy said to Wayne, "is what would happen if Deion Sanders say to Mickey Mantle, Run it out, you piece of shit homeboy!"

From his distance, Harry announced, "Mickey Mantle had bad knees, he never run shit."

"I *know* that," the black guy said. "That ain't my point."

"I get you point," Harry said. "All shit break loose is what happen."

The black guy raised his hand and Harry high-fived it. Wayne looked on.

Wayne said, "I don't understand Jesse Jackson *or* Mickey Mantle *or* Deion Sanders."

"I believe that," the black guy said, and looked to Harry for another high five, but Harry declined. Wayne bought the round and Harry served the beers and neatened everything up. Wayne didn't know why he wanted to talk to the black guy in the first place, except he was sure the guy was a roofer and Wayne would be needing a job, but he didn't need a job this soon, so he didn't know why he started talking to the black guy, roofer or not, but now he had a buzz and didn't mind talking to him.

"Hey!" he suddenly said. "You mean this thing where Carlton Fisk says to Deion Sanders, Run it out, you piece of shit or something?"

The black guy and Harry exchanged glances.

"Einstein," the black guy said.

"Git it, git it, git it, guitar *Sam!*" Wayne shouted. "I get it now."

"Get my man a beer," the black guy said. "That is one *trazee* white man."

"That is John Wayne," Harry said.

"*Wayne*, Stone," Wayne said to the black guy.

"Robert Williams," the black guy said to Wayne. "Don't call me Bob." Wayne and Robert Williams shook hands clumsily, Wayne attempting a black shake and Robert Williams a white shake. The fumbling resulted in Wayne chuckling and a white shake.

"So they hiring where you are?" Wayne asked.

"What day is this?"

"Friday."

"Monday will be Monday, right?"

"Stoweno."

"It's roofing, right?"

"Water runs downhill and wet things don't stick together."

"They hiring."

Wayne had a pair of the most bleached-out blue eyes Robert Williams had ever seen. It was hard to maintain, drunk or not, that those eyes could be connected to the devil. In fact, when Robert Williams shook Wayne's hand, thinking it an act of racial duplicity, he was surprised to receive from Wayne a current of no malice whatsoever. Wayne was a new kind of blue-eyed devil: one who could not say *nigger* with sufficient heat or conviction to be anything but comical or innocently self-referential. What Robert Williams felt, despite himself, when he shook the fumbling, dirty hand of this Cloroxed pinkish devil was a small surge of pity.

On Monday morning at Ponderosa Roofing and Sheet Metal Robert Williams spoke highly of Wayne's credentials as a roofer and Wayne was hired.

[After securing his position at Ponderosa Roofing and Sheet Metal, which also manufactured, it turned out, serious roofing equipment, for which Wayne thought he could be a sales representative, particularly for the gas-powered gravel scarifier, as it was properly called, or power spudder, as it was known by those who used it, Wayne went on a date. There was a woman in the office named Pamela Forktine and Wayne could not resist asking her every morning for plastic spoons for the coffee-stirring operations, which were prodigious operations at Ponderosa or any other roofing company at six in the morning among troops as hungover and blear—their brogans flared open at the untied ankles and sticking to the floor, their flannel shirts not altogether tucked in, their hair wet-combed—as the troops at Ponderosa or any roofing company.

Wayne said, "Spoons, Ms. Forktine. Ms. Forktine, spoons." Pamela Forktine was older than Wayne. She had put up with the advances of every description of loser testosterone hardcase it was conceivable to put up with, until Wayne. Wayne was to her mind so far gone on rancid testosterone he was sweet. That her fifteen or so years on him did not seem to bother him—a direct result, as she saw it, of the hormonal dementia these boys suffered—made her certain he was sweet.

The fifteen or so years she had on him did *not* bother Wayne, until they went out and Pamela Forktine took the bull by the horns and said, while they were going counter-clockwise in their cowboy boots and she was looking for Wayne's chest hair between the pearl snaps of his shirt with her finger, "You want to do the bone dance?"

"Do *what*?" Wayne said, stopping their counter-clockwise drift among the stream and creating eddies of resentment on the floor around them. "I mean, *sure*," he said, and they got going again.

"It's what kids say," Pamela Forktine said. "Bone in, bone out."

Wayne sort of bent over at the waist, blowing his nose at this. He turned a red far deeper than the yoke on his shirt. He had a piece of ass, it was a lock, but this kind of talk embarrassed him to a dangerous point. If Pamela Forktine wanted to do the bone dance, then Pamela Forktine had best not say anymore about it.

They went to her house. There she scared Wayne by looking in another room and announcing, "It's okay. He's out."

"Who?"

"Rafe."

"Rafe?"

"Oh. Raphael."

"Who's Raphael?"

"My son."

"How old is he?"

"Nineteen." Pamela Forktine had led Wayne into the living room and was making them a drink in the kitchen. Wayne pondered getting beat up by a nineteen-year-old kid named Raphael. His original concern had been that Pamela Forktine was married and that he might be shot by a Mr. Forktine. That was, now, preferable to this other. Raphael Forktine was either going to be a homosexual of some sort or some kind of terminator. *Rafe Forktine* sounded like death row.

When he looked back on it, picturing Pamela Forktine's death-row-candidate son beating the ever-living shit out of him might have been the high point in the travail of his and Pamela Forktine's eminent time together. But Rafe Forktine did not burst in and rescue Wayne from what was about to happen. No one did, including God.

Before God and everybody else, Pamela Forktine walked in the room with two drinks and her blouse open, no bra. This required of Wayne a careful, very casual double take. Her breasts were not altogether visible because they seemed to point down and away from each other, like a cartoon hound dog's eyes. It was the end of subtlety on Pamela Forktine's part. "Where's that bone, Wayne?"

Wayne turned red and made a splitting noise.

"In here?" Pamela Forktine made one stroking pass, one unzipping pass, and scared Wayne with an immediate and vigorous program of what he would later term *gobbling*. It included a gobbling noise. Wayne would have laughed but was too frightened. The gobbling worked, though, and Pamela Forktine got up very cuddly in his neck, her knees facing him on the sofa, and said, "Oh, sweetie. I hope I'm okay."

"You're okay, *sure* you're okay—"

"No, I mean. Well. I've been . . ."

This scared Wayne again. "You've been . . . what?"

"Dry."

"What?"

"I've been, well, *dry*."

There they were in a brightly lit living room waiting for a nineteen-year-old son to avenge his mother, who said things like *bone in bone out*, gobbled you, was dry. Wayne was about to lose it. Why did pussy have to be this way? Why could it not be like in a magazine? Like in a book? Like at least in *a story*, something that went smooth and *worked*.

But Pamela Forktine was not giving up. She gobbled, she got Wayne into the bedroom, she got on Wayne, and Wayne had a passing fancy that her hair felt like hemp rope and her skin like party balloons three days after the party. But this felt good, this harsh rope and loose satin, and made its opposite number, fine hair and young tight flesh, seem like tomatoes and eggplants, and Wayne began if not gobbling back at least nibbling this satiny crinkly Pamela Forktine, and Pamela Forktine, when that didn't tickle too much, seemed to like it and kept saying "Oh, sweetie" and was not dry. It worked. Wayne gasped up on her like a shipwrecked man on his found island. "Oh, sweetie, sweetie, sweetie," Pamela Forktine said, patting his head in rhythm.

This was a very sad and silly business, Wayne thought, this woman calling him this for not doing any more than not losing his desire and spooing in her in five minutes, but she was calling him this *sweetie* nonsense without any joke, she was serious, and that made Wayne feel, despite himself, good. She could by God call him whatever she wanted to. What had she ever done to him? She had *fucked* him, that's what, and that was what he'd asked for. He was going to be man enough to take what he got if he was man enough to ask for it.

And he was asking for it, man or not. *Man.* God, or whoever, put you here, and you *have* to ask for it. He puts water here and it *has* to run downhill. You get up there in fucking 120-degree heat and have to stop its running. You fix the fucking leak.

"I sprung a leak in you, Pamela Forktine," Wayne said.

"You sure did."

"Was it too soon?"

"No, sweetie. It was just fine."

Just fine, Wayne knew, meant too soon. So what? Was that his fault? No, it was not. Water runs downhill. It has to.

—

It was not a new beginning, but it was, Wayne thought, new enough. He was half asleep and inadvertently said, aloud, "New enough," and Pamela Forktine said, "Hmm? Did you say nude enough?"

"Sounds like a wiener," Wayne said.

They nestled and snuggled together. Pamela Fork-tine said, "Do you like cereal? Rafe likes cereal. You can stay. There's enough."

"There's nude enough?"

"Nude enough."

It was their first joke together. Wayne said, "I had a twin brother no one knows about. Sparky. Sparky died and Wayne lived."

"I'm sorry, sweetie. How old was he?"

"Sparky was three. Minutes."

"Mmmm."

"Nude enough."

"I'm nude enough, Wayne."

"What? More?"

"Sounds like a wiener, sweetie."

Wayne liked women who said what they wanted. Up to a point. This was the point. This was precisely the point. He liked Pamela Forktine.

———

Wayne took, as he puts it, a dump. This came out of him loose and burning. It made him step more highly than usual for a few minutes afterward and wish for some kind of soothing salve. "Is there any beer?" he asked Pamela Forktine. This was probably a mistake, at nine in the morning with a new woman with a teenage son possibly already in the kitchen eating cereal. Next he would be watching cartoons. Wayne gave this some thought. Maybe this was not the place to be.

Pamela Forktine had not heard him, apparently,

and he heard no noise in the kitchen, so he tiptoed in there and looked, and there was no beer. He went back in the bathroom and closed the door and looked at himself in the mirror. His hair was dirty and it had the kind of control to it that suggested someone had jerked large chunks of it out. Except it was so greasy how could anyone get a *grip* on it? Wayne did this himself—grabbed a chunk of hair—and felt it slipping in his hand well before it hurt to pull it. He thought about a shower. That might constitute a moving-in gesture—he did not want that. And he did not want this Rafe character, convict or cartoon-watcher cereal-eater, to find him in the shower the first time they met.

He looked at himself again. His face was, as all faces are to their owners, inscrutable. It was "normal" up to a point. It had high, glossy, rather boyish cheeks and a freckled nose, not too veined, and the always slightly burned forehead was plain. Then the trouble started. That wild skyline of hair and, when he smiled, something that gave Wayne the willies, like mold on cheese gave him the willies, because you never knew, once you got away from outright yellow cheese into cheese that was white, or nearly white, it could be bluish or greenish, and soft, you never knew *how* soft until you touched it— once you got away from yellow cheese you did not know if the mold was mold or part of the cheese itself. That was the feeling he had, looking at his teeth in Pamela Forktine's mirror, on a Saturday morning. He looked around the bathroom: it was good old tile, black and white, and she had knickknack shelves everywhere and all the towels and face towels neatly hung, and the toilet was covered in carpet that matched the rug on the floor. He smiled at himself quickly and got the blue-cheese willies and got in the shower anyway.

He soaped up very, very well and took two or three kinds of shampoo from a rack of them, whether they said Conditioner or not, or Oily or Dry or Normal, and washed everything hard and got a boner. All right. He was back. The killer was back.

[**W**ayne has set out an aluminum-framed plastic-webbed chaise lounge in the large gravel beside Lake Travis. He gets in the lounge, has him a Coors in one hand and a cigarette in the other, takes a drag and a drink, says, "Ahhhhh . . . The only thing I need now is for some broad to give me a knobber." He grins seedily, seedily the only way you can grin if your teeth appear to have small black-and-green flies on them. "A blonde," he adds.

Another drag on the cigarette and a *long* pull on the Coors. It does not pay to drink a beer slowly in this heat.

Wayne is pleased with himself. A knobber indeed. Why should Wayne not get a knobber? Why should he? The first question is the one Wayne would entertain if he were to entertain one of them. He won't. He will entertain only the positive if slight prospect of reclining in the sun beside his rod and reel baited for catfish, drinking a cold beer, not working on a roof, smoking a cigarette, and having a woman, preferably blond, give him a knobber, as he puts it.

Why should he? is the question that only others entertain at this juncture. If he indeed induced a woman to oblige his need, and should a fish manifest, you can see him leaping out of the chair, and out of her mouth, to tend his rod. Should his fiberglass rod, propped on a forked stick driven into the lake gravel, but twitch, Wayne would be there. Missing the fish, as he would, despite his three-time hook-set philosophy, which he is willing to articulate and demonstrate even while losing fish, Wayne would resume his position on the lounge with a fresh beer and say, addressing the blonde still on her knees in the gravel, "Missed him. Okay."

Thus the question: Can Wayne expect a knobber from a beautiful blonde in the rightful world? And the world's answer is no.

But Wayne has an advantage over the rightful world. Wayne is certain that he is himself. It is a weak, quivering self, afraid of nearly everything on earth, but Wayne knows it.

—

Wayne rebaits. Takes one pretty-good-looking chicken heart off his hook and tosses it to the gravel, where ants will find it in about ten minutes, though there is not an ant on the beach, and puts a better-looking chicken heart on, a fresh purple-red cone with a band of yellow fat on it, and casts it out, *far like he can*, as he puts it in his Mexican English. To cast out as far like he can is farther than he should, because the fish, if there are any, are in closer. But Wayne is the kind to speak perennially of "the channel," of the necessity of casting into this channel, which is never marked—you have *to know*—but is always, wherever you fish, far out there, at precisely the distance Wayne can cast if he casts far like he can.

[**F**loyd, Wayne's brother, still lives with his and Wayne's mother. Floyd is a large, soft fellow who somehow is not regarded as *fat*, or quite grown, which is why, probably, at thirty-seven, people do not kill him. He is found in the wee hours wearing plaid sports coats too large even for him, the pockets loaded with science-fiction paperbacks, verbally assaulting police officers. He is arrested, to be bailed out by his mother. He returns home, red-eyed, with his science-fiction books stacked neatly on his folded coat on his high knees during the front-seat ride home in his mother's car. She is not mad at him, or really worried. He's Floyd and he's home.

Wayne is putting his car in a ditch, putting Antabuse under his tongue, putting his kids in a motel to hide them from his wife, putting dollar bills in a jukebox at eleven in the morning, putting a chaise lounge beside a lake to call for an imaginary broad to give him a knobber. Wayne has thrown away everything except a folding plastic-and-aluminum chair, an Igloo Playmate cooler, and his cigarettes.

Floyd has thrown away nothing—not his childhood room, his toys in it, or his mother.

Mr. Stark, father and husband, threw them all away, one presumes.

Floyd is Mrs. Stark's boy.

Wayne is on his own.

Wayne inherited the throwing-away. Wayne even threw away the United States Navy. Once, an Ingersoll-Rand compressor, admittedly someone else's, but *still*.

Floyd? Asleep. Mrs. Stark is watching a late-morning soap. These people are afraid of nothing.

—

Floyd is talking, on a roof: "It was thirteen inches long and nine inches around—"

"On the soft?" Wayne asks.

"On the soft," Floyd says, with a giggle. "I think."

Wayne pulls out his tape measure and starts measuring roof jacks. As these things happen, the fourth or fifth jack—a lead jacket for open ventilation pipes protruding through roofs—is *exactly* thirteen inches high and nine inches around.

"If that son of a bitch has a dick *that* big," Wayne says, "you tell that son of a bitch I'll suck it."

Floyd giggles some more. "I don't know where he is."

"I thought he was your friend," Wayne says.

"My *friend's* friend."

"I don't care *who* the son of a *bitch* is. I'll suck it." Wayne measures another jack.

Wayne is serious in the one way Wayne can be serious: trivial outrage. He is being lied to, albeit thirdhand, about a ludicrous matter, but insofar as *Wayne* has a member that *he* cannot tell anyone is thirteen inches long by nine inches around—*on the soft*—he is outraged. The gentleman of mythic dimension has breached a protocol of manners, even for roofers, and Wayne will see him in a duel, if he can. Wayne proposes not to duel evenly, member-to-member; Wayne proposes false submission: he will contest this liar *on his knees*. The true beauty of this is that if the man did appear, up the ladder and over the horizon of the roof edge, carrying with him this great, leaden soil pipe between his legs, Wayne would not suck it. Wayne would turn profoundly red, giggling now himself—Floyd would stop giggling, at this point embarrassed and a little outraged to have delivered the goods, only to have his brother welsh—and begin *complimenting* the bearer of the cannon.

Wayne would say, "That's a goddamned *weenie!* That is a *goddamned weenie!*"

The man of course is never to be produced, and the day of measuring roof jacks and threatening the man declines from its prospects of gargantua, Wayne retiring to Coors, Floyd to science fiction. For weeks, even months, Wayne and Floyd measure roof jacks. A surprising number can be found that measure thirteen inches in height by nine inches in girth, exactly.

Wayne and Floyd measure roof jacks finally automatically, compulsively, learning to gauge them on sight with great precision—"Ten-seven, skip it"—and finding the eerily common thirteen-nine in a twilight zone of ambivalent sexuality. After work they clean themselves with creamy go-jo and coarse rags and cold beer.

Finally they stop measuring roof jacks. Wayne may shake his head occasionally, passing a thirteen-nine. Floyd ignores or has forgotten roof jacks as anything other than obstacles not to trip over.

Days, once they abjure gargantua, even absurd gargantua, and descend into their ordinary smallnesses, have a way of remaining small. The lives that inhabit the days also assume postures of ordinary smallness. One day an apex of sorts, laughable though it be, of men together measuring roof jacks with twenty-five-foot Stanley Powerlocks, gives way to the men scattered, disconnected, down from the roof, doing *less* than measuring roof jacks and laughing. Threatening nothing. Threatening, finally, not even themselves.

[**A**nd Wayne today? Wayne today is as elusive as Wayne yesterday. But Wayne isn't afraid of anything because he *knows* he is afraid of it. I, by contrast, think myself fearless, and when something scares me *it scares the shit out of me* and forces me to undergo a little private analysis the likes of which never trouble Wayne. If you are afraid of *everything*, you are finally not afraid of anything. It is when you presume to be *not* afraid of a few things that the terror creeps in. The terror resides in correctly identifying what you are afraid of and what you are not afraid of. The absolutely fearful person is in an absolute and comfortable position: against the ropes, ready for it all. The presumer, the poseur of courage, is looking left, right, behind himself, trembling.

And what of Ugly, Wayne's estranged wife, with two kids and already, no doubt, Wayne's bad teeth in their malnourished heads? What of poor Felicia and the rug rats? Plastic shoes, polyester shorts, impetigo legs, *happily playing*, and *at nothing* demonstrably inventive or clever or advanced or Montessori. The debilitating issue of debilitated parents. Who will grow up to be, the boys, broadcast magnates or serial killers and, were there girls, Union 76 cashiers or actresses of first-tier Hollywood sexuality. Life all over the road. These people are afraid of nothing.

Of Felicia I know nothing. On the one occasion when Wayne called her Ugly in my presence, I noticed at that moment her nice ass, in short, tight shorts of a color like magenta, set off by her very white legs and of a stretchy knit material, the combination of which— these dimestore pants and unhealthily white legs—was exciting, and if she had asked *me* if she was ugly, I would have said she was not, but she did not (why would she? how could she?), and I did not volunteer a correction (very easy to do: "Wayne, for God's sake"). And why did I not correct him? None of my business? Too smarmy? Would it have been open flirtation to compliment her even by the left-handedness of scolding my friend her husband? I think I suspected I would worsen the situation if I said, *Not ugly to me.* And this seems true still. But *how* I might have worsened it was obscure then and still is. Felicia would have given me a look, then or an hour later, delivered me a colder beer than that she delivered Wayne, or she would have been disgusted with me. That, I think, is the better probability. *Not ugly, big boy? And what are you going to do about it? Shit.* And she continues to diaper a rug rat, fetch us beer, hide.

I was perfectly free to say, "Wayne, if she's ugly, I'll tell you what: I'll pay your rent and bills here for a month and all I want is one week with her, *if* she'll have me. Put the question to her." I was perfectly free to do this. Of all the things I was afraid of, Wayne was not one of them.

At the time I would have seen such a proposition as a blessing, or at least an improvement, for the suffering Felicia. A week with me! All my teeth! Muscles! College! Now I see that she was lucky I never spoke.

Wayne may be roofing, but I am afraid.

[*All Along*

the Watchtower

Chihuahua

[Very often, every day, every so often, every day I go down to the quay. To the water. No quay. Don't know what a quay is.

Every day I go down to the water. I would like to say this. Every day I go down to the water.

Lies abound: not every day, not go down, and what precisely does "to the water" purport to mean? To lap it, to look at it, to get in it, all the above, none, what? And "the water"—what water, and if it were determinable would it be the *same* water every day? I think not.

I and some water on a daily basis come face-to-face; that is ridiculous but not more inaccurate. I entertain some wetness before me. But it is not really the water itself one goes down to, whether going down or up, which you might do were the water a volcano lake, and mine might be, my water, which is not mine to possess except in figure of speech; it is not the water to which one "goes" but its garnish. I fancy crabs, spiders that can walk on the water, rings on it made by the lips of fish snapping at spiders, though I glean that fish avoid the arachnid; water lily, lily pad, other kelpishness and rot, mud beside the water and under the water, the abandoned appliance in the water and in the mud, orphaned tackle, predators dead and alive, trash in the water, turtles. It is not the water but that for which the water is a vehicle that we go, however often, down to, or up to, to do what we do at the water. A redheaded neighbor named McGillicuddy, who looks and acts exactly like Lucille Ball, and I possibly mean Lucille Ball playing a character named McGillicuddy, which I think she did, and I wonder at this set of connections, if that they are, but not much, because I do not have time: this very real Mrs. or Ms. or Miss M. is after me. Her boy has a blue trike. Him I like. She has chased me, palpably.

Obloquy—what the hell does that mean? Are we a little tired of a lack of education here? I submit that I am. Yam.

Of indigo ravens near the water I am fonder than a two-stroke for oil. And some Juicy Fruit to watch them by, my my my. Paper clouds the issue. For me. There is litter in the world, most of it paper, some of it technically trash and some of it merely finally trash after a full life of not-trash, your contracts and books and things. They, too, finally litter the busied head. As much as a worm box a lakeshore. My head is a mudbank. Do not depend on me for your logic. You can depend on me to bitch about litter and head litter and to run from Mrs. McGillicuddy until she catches me, and that probably she probably will. Do. Oops. Oopsie-Daisy. What if that—Oopsie-Daisy—were her first name?

I have reason to suspect that Oopsie-Daisy McGillicuddy does not wear underwear for profit. She is a not-for-profit corpus chasing me uptown and down. I like the odd red sky by the water. I like the green wrinkled pea. I toured France as a teenager and had the runs and felt the women smelled not good and the men puffed much too much when they spoke, if you could call it that, and you could, French is a language. Water harbors mosquitoes, sort of; that is obvious but not in altogether obvious ways, all the time. I don't mind speaking the untruth when it can be had. That solid shit they hit down the fairway for centuries has been hit, and played, and now we all labor on divoted ground, ground under repair. Our heads still work, it's the course. The course has got too many people on it, and it should not have been opened to the public. Casual water—a good one.

I defer.

—

I have not and will not go to war. I have not and will not make money. I have not and will not break ranks with bourgeois order. I have not and will not have much fun, or much pain, in this tour of duty we will be forced to call my life. Is it sad, this not having? It might be, if one could actually think about the situation in its entirety, but if one could do that he would likely be able to engage in escaping the bourgeois board game.

What have I done, will I do? I will pay the bills, cure the ills, put on weight, engage in non-reproductive copulations with a degree of ardor that suggests a compensating for all the other, larger not having. Then it will end and some paper in my name will be redeemed and there will be a pleasant bit of change for survivors and having not wept much they will not celebrate much. They will spend it and I am gone, paper and all. How nice an idea the funeral pyre. How nice an idea the rain tire. How nice an idea chartered bus. How nice an idea large red soda waters and bad teeth. You have this, these in life. People are essentially uninteresting to each other and yet finally alien to each other to a degree that should make us all compelling of the minutest attention we can pay. But alas, we sleep the days, sometime prowl the nights, but groggily and in fits of self-interest only.

—

The little boy Tod's blue trike is in the bushes with me. Mrs. McGillicuddy is underwearless on her bed watching TV. She is slack and ope-legged and hairy and not ribald, and I do don't want to make a noise. Sitting on the seat of the blue trike is a carton, one pint, of chocolate milk, the thick dark heavy commercial glop that can be so good once every year or so. I open it and gently maneuver the trike out and ride it down the quiet street drinking my milk. It is milk of this sort that made the darker races dark, in this country. In others, where Nestlé, etc., has only so far purveyed baby formula, ivory in color, the sun or other natural forces have darkened the native. There is a cool breeze blowing across the fine sweat on my forehead as I relax into my crime and ride my stolen joyous wheels. The carton in its perdurable wax fortress will hold sufficient residue of chocolate and milk to lure in and somehow not let out a very large roach, who will die. But for now I am innocent, pedaling and waving at the imaginary crowd lining the parade route. Mrs. McGillicuddy, hirsute and hungry and pink-nightied, haunts me and gives my cheerful waves an abbreviated uncertainty and hesitation to let go the handlebars, where I've inadvertently, now the milk is done, gripped both hands for hard pedaling and speed.

When arrested I say only "California or bust" in answer to all questions and am held for psychiatric evaluation, which does not come to anything. I go every day down to the water. Every day to the water, down or up or over or across or proximate or nearly or mostly or delicately or boldly or trepidously or joyously or sadly or bummeduply or downtroddenly or upbeatly or stealthily or healthily or lamely or gamely, I go. I take my time.

I bide it. I tried it. I tried time out and did not like it. It's not for me. It asks too much of you. There is the incarcerated meaning of it and of course the "free" version of it. Sapling, I mean *sampling*, them both in my time, I find the incarcerated a cinch to manipulate and the free a bitch. No. Impossible. Free time is like a grizzly bear of disorder, multiple weapons all on a scale of destruction so large you do not even properly, by which I mean rationally, have time—well, that is obvious, that is my point here—have the wherewithal to begin to cope or adjust or posture for its advent and its certain eating you alive, timelessly, in about no time at all—that's free time. Just bide it. Ride hide slide it. Deride it. Chide it, elide it, take pride in it, decide within it you've got to abide it, confide in it, be beside yourself in it, collide with it, tempocide in it. Triking down the street on Tod McGillicuddy's trike I should have been charged with tempocide but was charged with malicious mischief— same thing—instead.

I go at or down on the water every day, except some days. Some days I lie on it like a compass needle and point eventually north. This is a function of magnetism and of getting on the water very very easily. Surface co-hesion must exceed the water's affinity for you. The wa-ter has no real affinity for you, and prefers that you merely lie on top of her rather than getting in, but you must cooperate by gently gently slowly slowly getting on, *easy*. I dig that, that I dig. With your head true north you can begin to think.

—

In the Sahara night your clothes tend to bubble off you. This is not so for all the women on safari with you. Discretion.

I go down to the water and make arithmetic in the mud. A calculus of sneaker toe. No, I but figure the com-pensation due Tod McGillicuddy for the (unauthorized) loan of his trike. It was impounded at the arrest and lost. The police lost Tod McGillicuddy's trike. What wonder we have a problem with law and order. I set my mind to repay the little squirt and it came out funny. I had a trust formed in his name and a Harley-Davidson delivered to their driveway. Its reception I watched through the blinds. Tod seemed not quite to get it but his mother was excited. She wheeled it with some difficulty into the garage, which is served by an electric door. The bike was magnificent in the sun: full rakes gleaming in their ridiculous thrust, absurd tiny sexy pearl-drop gas tank, small double-decker leather seat, and titty grips of some gauzy open-celled foam I did not, but wanted to, feel before Mrs. M. put the monster away. No questions, no looking around in wonder, just secure the motorcycle, and Tod doesn't look at it twice. Tod, my boy.

—

I'm whiling away some convalescent time, simple private recovery time you need after mental incarceration. It, that, being held for want of mind, suspected alleged want of mind, is thrilling: it is like going to the circus when you are young, except you are not young and you *are* the circus, and the doctors and the police are very young and they are watching you perform. Thrilling, this reversal, and a bit exhausting, which is why drugs are contraindicated in cases of mind watch, in my book, my small unmanly book. They lay Thorazine on you and you partake of the bear who runs over the trainer on the bicycle and no one can ever tell from the bear's expression if he meant to do it or not, but everyone is happy to speculate for years, generally of course informing the bear with motives of vengeance as people seeing trained bear are wont, oh so wont, to do, I'm tired. An odd tear runs from my right eye as I convalesce and glance the street for Tod.

Why I resist Mrs. M.'s wanton desire for me I do not know, except that the proposition of someone looking like Lucille Ball coming after you without the talent or the money of Lucille Ball takes some getting used to, and actually *Lucille Ball*, as opposed to characters played by, is right good-looking, stunning even, but no one thinks this when he thinks of Lucy in her many incarnations. I submit: after Judy Garland in *Oz*, the national male psyche is rooted most firmly to Lucy. This is why Mrs. M. scares me, like toys you recall you lost over the years without knowing how and realizing they're worth a fortune now—I'd like to know how my arrowheads and coin collections for God's sake got away from me. Who would throw those away? Would your mother throw away your arrowheads and your *coin* collection? What wonder they let us go to Vietnam or wherever else big-eared Texans pretend we must. Then they bitch, of course, but you're dead by the time they discover the Communist menace not to have been altogether germane. And you are no hero yourself, you also arrowheadless coinless little fyce who have had time in your ignoble pinball childhood to gobble up large portions at the table of national humanistic bunk—you are down there at induction, coughing gingerly so you don't herniate yourself out of the chance of getting killed in order to protect your mother, who has thrown away your toys. Well, I have a piece of advice for you, me so narrowly just on mind watch: Fuck your mother. That's the first thing to do here, fuck your mother and get on with it. All part of why Mrs. M. has got a headlock on me and all she wants is a liplock.

—

Sunny, fair, down-to-the-water cloudy, I go. My pants are fitting not well, my shoes seem askance independent of my feet, I hear the odd wailing noise in one ear. I fancy eating some sugar, good crystalline gob of it partially dissolved in thin coffee. One of those two-stage plastic cup-and-base rigs be nice, white cup like a space capsule, detaches for orbit into the garbage when the bum they've sold it to is through with it down to the Krispy Kreme. Yessiree, I'ma headed down to the water for a doughnut and a very white plastic cup of coffee, which I will be allowed nay expected to call by some hip street appellative: *Give me a cup o' that java, miss, some o' that mud, tee-hee.* Life.

Use of this product may be hazardous to your health—I read on the door to the Jules Vermin Studio of Dance. So I went in. There were floor marshals from ACE and Civil Defense around the floor, and the couples were belted together and helmeted and wearing boxing groin guards. They stepped only on painted yellow footprints on the floor. It was explained by a taped message playing repeatedly that a certain kind of neck strain might result from looking constantly at the footprints but that this was preferable to the kinds of injuries that would result from looking up. No one looked up. The marshals seemed satisfied, most satisfied. I suddenly wanted to eat some Japanese food and retired from the Jules Vermin Studio without receiving any instruction. And knew in a vision that were Mrs. M. and I ever to dance it would be in the moonlight and we would not watch where we were going. How hard to do, I thought, but how obvious it is that you should live every day as though you are dying. Why do only brain-tumor folk seem to actually get on this with any arguable grip?

Them and, say, junkies. Them and junkies and, say, preachers. Them and junkies and preachers and, say, people who want you to invest in their real-estate scam? And the ACE marshals want you to live as if this is *not* the last day of your life. Why, it occurs to me to ask, does anybody care how I live my life? First, last, what is it to you? Who are you? If you are fired up about how I live this day, what are you doing with yourn? That what I wantn know. I talkn funny, so what. I been sick. When you sick you say things. You say things today you might not be able to say tomorrow. You say things today you might not be able to say tomorrow when you not sick, people say you a artist. People say you a artist you say anything come to mind or come to not mind. Ray Charles, boy. Thing come to mind, say it; thing come to not mind, say it. Not mind be body? Thing come to body, say it; body catch a body comin' thew the rye. Nobody got the leapest idea what rye is anymore, might as well say if a body catch a body comin' thew the prom.

I believe in many things, none of which comes to mind. I am in arrears pillwise.

—

I am a demographer in the demopolis. I am of a fragile solidity, like Aristotle. I—

—

Lord, how time flies when the tourniquet is on. Little Tod M.'s big old hog breathes idle in his garage. I been down but not like this before. You don't shoe horses without their walking on your back. The bluebottle fly is a thing of the past. Tawdry sentiments dress like women. People behave like their mothers. I'm down to my last dime. Forever is a chute of bugs in a thimble of sense. Sweeteners go to hell. Be patient, my pretty, the sandman uses the postal service just like everybody else wears his pants. Downtown it is holy. Before the Lord has had his way He will have slept. Before time began there was no money. Now they say time is money. I refute that. Anybody could.

——

Anybody could do anything, and sooner or later everybody has. It's a mess and I'm hungry. The womb has to dilate before people can get out. They in there saying "Hep me!" behind a *sphincter*. My knowledge of medicine does not exceed that of the average layman. Of this I am proud. I know doctors whose knowledge of medicine does not exceed that of a layman and I would as soon not be associated with them. If anyone suggests there's a goddamned thing wrong with eating soft bread, he is not a doctor. I fell hard as a child for the fiery hot non-chewable gumball, or it wasn't a gumball—*gum*ball—must have been called a jawbreaker. They were a fine invention on the plane of human non-necessity, on which plane we need more play. I am probably a classical anarchist, but have no classical education or manners. Blue porcelain that is not too delicate is a good thing. A hayride with a buxom laughing lass of East European stock is a good thong, I mean thing. Drinking some wine and ravishing her should she want that, also. If she does not, hail fellow well met and get out of the wagon in a good homey spray of moonlight and be of good cheer. She should be, too. If she is not, attribute it to the rotten modern world along with everything else that rightly *dispiace*. The stray straw on your person brush incompletely off entering the solid, below-grade, amber-lit tavern that warmly invites you to its bosom for the night. Say practical things, and not an abundance of them, to the company of the evening. Do not discuss annuities or topics such as that. Be hearty and agreeably tired, like everyone else behaving himself. That is a good mantra, not just tonight but always: *I want us all to behave ourselves* (chuckle).

—

I am withering on the vine of the afternoon of my afterlife, having consumed my afterbirth. Et my own. Became perennially hungry. Mrs. M. I am afraid is at the door. Glowering:

—What is the matter with you?

—Madame, what is not?

—You a pederast? Throws hip out.

—I have many faults, and some I do not know about, but that inclination is not among the known or the unknown, I fain. (She appears mollified, to soften; I am encouraged to issue some more.) Though we would be remiss not to entertain what Coleridge intended to say when he spoke of things visible and not in the universe: people, he tried to say—but couldn't because the Romantic Age disallowed the diction, let alone the sentiment—people are much more a piece of shit than not a piece of shit—

Mrs. M. has slammed the door and left. I can't afford to worry the matter of her errant accusation, truly ungrounded, any more than one can afford to worry the matter of exclusion from jury duty. Whatever else may be said about the modern world, you can securely say that if you are seated on a jury today there is something irretrievably wrong with you and at least one team of lawyers, who are troubled themselves, knows it.

Had dog, dog died. Been in stir, got out. I think sometimes of lovely things, the slender turquoise glass on a white table in the black room. There is nothing else in the room. There is not the mateless sock, the canned-ham can in the plastic garbage pail, the torn mail, the carpet, the lowering ceiling, the mortgaged walls, the crudescence of life, the chaff of slow daily dying (unsolicited credit-card applications). Only the aqua vase on white on black, no flower necessary to behold its beauty. A large fire needs be set around the vase. That is house-cleaning beyond the tolerances of the bourgeois.

—Then why don't you *ask me out*!

Mrs. M. has burst back in. And burst back out before I can answer. Which is good: all I have in mind to utter is How's Tod's bike? Which for all I know Mrs. M. is eating piece by piece in her Genie-guarded hot garage. There is a fine long red hair hanging from the doorknob. It lifts gently away and around the room in its random reach, not unlike a tentacle. A tentacle of rosy doom from the nice lonely octopus across the street. It is time, perhaps, for burglar bars.

—

Because once you decide anything, nothing is possible. Because . . . So I decided to hit the dusty trail, which is not dusty and not a trail but a web of human snail paths of mucus in the considerably lapsed garden. I had an appointment of sorts at the halfway house, where the sheriff expected me to surrender myself after I watered my plants, or some such nonsense I'd made up during the incarceration *pro tem.* I took some pills someone had prescribed and called Safety Cab and was met at the curb at dawn by the curiously agreeable purring, smoking cold cab driven by the curiously agreeable, smoking, cold cabdriver wearing his leather jacket and sporting his earthly wisdom. "I am supposed to go to Tacachale, but take me to the airport."

"I got you. Wouldn't go to Taco Charley's my own self."

And with chuckles all around, stopping at the Sprint store for coffees so large it takes two hands to negotiate them so my man at the wheel has to use a straw, we head for aeroporto. We pass the very hospital they expect me at: a fully respectable mental hospital once called Sunland now uplifted by the AmerIndian moniker—is the suggestion here that *Indians* had mental problems? That they *deserve* to have large holding pens of adult retards named after them?—Tacachale. In two minutes it was renamed on the street of political skepticism Taco Charley's. I was altogether calmed by my resolve to disregard.

"Naw," my driver is saying, shaking his head and sipping his straw as we pass the compound. "You don't look like no burrito to me." The fix is in: Why do I not go to Mexico? Isn't that the place for me? I do don't see why not.

Allow me to explain a few things. It is not altogether unfitting that They want to have a look at me in the burrito bin. That much even you know given the little . . . dog trotting down the street. But I argue that once you let Them single you out, arbitrarily electing *not* to lock up every other person in the world today, all of whom necessarily belong in there with you, including Them, of course, which is why They have positioned Themselves at the front of the room with the clipboards and the whistles, you have allowed a gross injustice and you should not go gentle into that nightie. So go to Mexico. That is where I want to go.

"I want to locate me a fifty-pound Chihuahua," I tell my driver, Nat. "Nat, I could stop the world I had me a fifty-pound Chihuahua."

"Know you could." He laughs. "Definitely stop it wid *dat*!" We are tee-hee tee-hee in the getaway car, enjoying the odd, scant pretense of racial harmony. ("Some cracker bust out Taco Charley's get in the cab today? He gone go to Mexico, he say, get him a *fitty-poun'* Chihuahua dog!" "What you do?" "Put him on the plane!" "Heard that!") The whole goddamned world has gone into ten-four good buddy, give or take some melanin. I am not a Royalist, but I would not mind being the King. Is all. Have me some purlieu around the castle, and these lurcher dogs what hold the trespasser down, without hurting him but scaring the potty training out of him until the King's men get there with the Pampers and the cuffs. In those days this lurcher dog hold down a man trying to get your deer; today a man will break in to eat your potato chips. Well he will certainly break in to eat your deer also, if you have it, but more likely you don't. More likely you are not the King. The King more likely has marital problems, or something, a hole in the trailer floor. I have tried to live a good, clean, cogent life, but it has been hard, and I do not think the fault lies with me. Some people seem to know things, and I am not among them. Not among the people who seem to know, not in the seeming know. Not. Airport. *Brokers*, for example, *lawyers*. Don't they just ooze with knowing? Their entire Being says, You don't know. You take your psychoanalyst, by contrast a learned man who at least has the dignity to say, Tell me about it, there's *some* things in your messed-up head I don't know. And well, once you blubber them he of course knows all about it and then is paid to ooze his knowing in controlled dribble all over your prostrate grateful form, fishing out your money, but still he does not answer the phone: "Freud, Jung. Will you hold?" AeroMexico. Via *Fort* Worth. Get me some spurs en route. Spurs and sunblock, all I need, and a copy of *Dog World*.

—

Got me a set of sandals made from tires, arc of tread and some rubber-coated cable, look good for about another twenty thousand miles. Got these from a man in Matamoros walked on his knees on the same sandals; I know these are good sandals. I have sold my wardrobe by haggling with a boy over the price of a carved bird and a yo-yo while another boy selling his sister ran off

with my valise—one calls it a valise if of European ex-
traction and relieved of it in non-Europe. This I know,
even if the odd American on the run from Taco Charley's
hardly qualifies. I got a red-striped shirt, or undershirt,
that invokes a comic character in low Italian opera. I
have never seen an opera. Does that matter? I am on the
lam and *it feels good*. I dyed my hair red. Actually, I put
a bottle of peroxide on it and before I got on the bus
good it was red and seems to have arrested there. I look
not unjustly like Mrs. M.'s husband, had she one. She
has sent her deprived need warping after me. She's in for
a certain disappointment, for this husband looks dis-
tinctly homosexual. And I already have wondrous sear-
ing hallucinatory dysentery, a truly fevered poop. I feel
like Zebulon Pike, of whom I know not one fact, and that
I say I feel like him has as much to do with me and his
ghost as with any nitpicking biographers who want to
challenge us. Those who choose to are free to challenge
a dead man with his name on a mountain if they want to.
There is not going to be a lot of challenging *me* from
here on in. I am bound for Chihuahua with a icee on my
knee. Don't you cry for me, I am bound for Chi-hoo-wa-
wa with my *Dog World* on my knee.

—

There are more important matters than Chi-
huahuas, fifty pounds or otherwise. I like the open window and a breeze. Inclemency is important. Dolls and
their effects on children, not to mention adults. Fiscal
policies, particularly those that oppress the indigent,
are "more important" than the fifty-pound Chihuahua.

Violations of human dignity in general and in all forms are "more important" than a dog, however spectacular it may be with its apple-dome cranium and wide-set bugged eyes and tiny feet and nervous happy prancing mince, looking, at fifty pounds, like a Doberman on nicotine and steroids. Yet for me no human concern is worth a damn next to the matter of a fifty-pound Chihuahua. Only *my wanting one* is on scale, in terms of human gravity, with the fifty-pound Chihuahua itself.

The bus I ride with my rubricated hair is all colors, I noticed getting on. It appears to have been perpetually painted, like a ship, but unlike a ship the bus is painted with whatever is at hand. It looks industrial hippie, naturally a tad garish but not deliberately so, in the interest of preservation rather than political statement. It is a scrambled color chart shambling and rusting withal down the dusty trail, which here is a dusty, mighty dusty trail, yessirreebob. Even the chickens in the good seats are hunkered down in their necks looking to be having difficulty breathing. The five men who entertained me by indiscreetly passing a switchblade back and forth among them are now not disapprovingly passing among themselves, taking swigs after studying the label, my bottle of peroxide, which I offered by way of greeting. Calloused feet abound, and the bloodshot eye, and the patient mostly overweight Madonna, and the knotty, fly-on-sore, rather-more-mucusy-than-not Child. And the squinting Chicken. And the open-eyed Me. Yes, Me, a virtual sunflower of perceptive acquisitiveness bouncing in full mental jacket on the bus with everybody else destitute enough to be in northeast Mexico without any prospects of visiting the beauty parlor or clocking in or calling the travel agent or writing the proposal or calling the agent or going to the doctor or the theater very soon. No, we are riding the bus; for now we are riding the bus. The Switchblades will find a 99-bottles-of-beer-on-the-wall pulque bar, the Chickens aroost in the dark where they will keep one eye open, the Madonnas a place to bed the sluggish Children and conceive some more. And I want a Dog.

—

There was a time when I was not this way. But: was there not such a time for us all? Do we not all claim a moment before which we were not the ruint sons of bitches we have become? Do you want or need to hear of my unfallen state when you have your own? I think not. Let us get on with it. I like a rigorous schedule of mental and physical exercise which cannot be adhered to, and good cotton socks and good leather boots. That is all I need, and the dog. Mysticism is a sport that any good failed scientist of the West can be a good amateur in by simply breathing his normal empirical air and not worrying too much about his (inevitable) failure (at science). I have found a candy bar in my seat on the bus and am looking around to see what might be the consequences of eating it. I feel like I've found a case of cigarettes in a penitentiary. The bus is cool and the candy firm. I do not recognize the brand. It is probably Nestlé in disguise. Or Coke. Nothing is simple. Capitalist raptors fly at seat level through the people's bus. I fall on my candy bar like a hero falling on a grenade. It's not bad, nutty with a bouquet of gasoline and lint.

—

We had a bus break and I got two chocolate-drink soda things, like the Yoo-Hoo in the States, but these look less, well, homogenous, more *cacciatore*. When I got back on the bus, one of the switchblade fellows was across my seat, with his feet in the aisle and his eyes slitted open to watch me react. I made a hand gesture that meant nothing, but amused his peers, and sat with a woman I know now to be a nurse. I offered her one of the coagulate Yoo-Hoos and to my surprise she accepted it, and to my further surprise she palmed me a pill, and to my further surprise I downed it, and to my further surprise it made me high in a solid quality oxycodone way. I was sorry to see the last of my runny Yoo-Hoo go. The bus was now winding precariously up into hills, and the livestock was restless, some of it running under the seats, and the tired civility of the folk was degrading into a workaday funk lending less charm to their colorful polyester clothes than you might have perceived had you been, say, a housewife from Oshkosh watching them get on the bus back in Matamoros and not getting on yourself but crossing back over the border in your rental car and sleeping the happy sleep of the well traveled in the TraveLodge with the sleepy-bear logo outside in calming neon and trademark-registered, waking once in the night when your husband suddenly was not beside you but relaxing immediately when he emerged from the bathroom, knowing it was his one nightly relief and that one at his age indicates no prostate alarum unless you are talking to the Cancer Society people, who tend to go overboard, but understandably, you suppose, and the nurse leaned to me as if falling asleep, and in fact had her head on my shoulder for a moment before she said, "Joo can come home me but do not see me your thing." I nodded vigorously at this suggestion, oddly cheered by her directness, and very suddenly rather depressed by the paucity of my knowledge of Mexico and the paucity of my business being in it. What I knew: the name Zapata, which I was not sure was Mexican; the name Bolívar, ditto; Santa Ana, definite, but a large loser; Cortés wrecked somebody (Peru?) (Where does Pizarro fit in?); Aztec-Mayan mess, some Egyptian-like outfits without mathematics and not sure where they were; one word: *perro*, dog, but I also thought it might mean *but* (and I dearly hoped not, because finding a fifty-pound *but* was going to be at once easier and more complicated than finding a fifty-pound dog); and that Trotsky had been assassinated in Mexico City, which I got, with an ice ax, which I did not get. That was the sum of Mexico as I sat going home with a nurse in my quest for a large Chihuahua. All in all, it was a fair fix. If I kneecapped the first switchblade boy off the bus with my Yoo-Hoo bottle it might command the respect of the others. Then I could make a dignified retreat to the pill-filled lair of my wanton health-care professional and have a very nice evening at home. I could relish her want of material overcomforts, her spare rooms free of the blued noise of TV, her hard mattress, one sheet, two cups, two plates. Her red table and matching yellow chairs. Her one strand of beads, her butt.

If she saw me it. I could go out late for two more

Yoo-Hoo, who knew. The world was opening up at this pinched lost end of it, opening up about a centimeter, but opening up.

We de-bused and the knife brigade came out, too, but were stopped by a vigorous look from the nurse, and one of them muttered *Strega* or something and they took off arunnin'. There was one other thing I knew about Mexico: some of the villages are inhabited by the dead. This I knew. Instinctively at first I hoped this village was not one of them, but then thought maybe that would be perfect, whatever that means, and what I think it means is you catch yourself in a dread common emotion and momentarily revolt: who in his right mind would prefer a village of normal Mexicans to one of the dead, on a purely anthropological basis, or perhaps forensic basis; the pill and the Yoo-Hoo had me going, and I put my arm around the nurse and we walked homeward looking like Mickey Rooney and a new wife. The thing is, I was *feeling* like Mickey Rooney with a new wife, and what I do not know about the emotions of Mickey Rooney is considerably less than what I do not know about those of Zebulon Pike, so we are on pretty firm ground. Mickey Rooney is the fifty-pound Chihuahua of actors, and that will do.

As casually as I could, I asked the nurse as we neared her place, "Is this a dead village?"

"Berry dead," she said.

—

Inside, it was exactly as I had pictured it, except for the presence of a complex and shining Cuisinart on the red table. The nurse turned to me and blinded me in a rush of cinnamon and chocolate tones. I had no chance to show her my anything. I felt vaguely unfaithful somehow to Mrs. M. and specifically furious with myself for such a sloppy emotion. I owed Mrs. M. nothing and certainly had repaid Tod a thousandfold for the use of his lost trike. How, I wondered, supine on a hard, comfy pallet looking at a moonlit countryside outside a window I expected a zombie to window-peek us through any minute now, for we were gloriously naked and ashine with exertion, my health-care professional resting her head on the hollow of my neck, how could a grown man's casual ride on a borrowed tricycle come to haunt so much of his life?

"Aches 'n' pains?" my nurse said.

"Oh yes," I said with the conviction of fatigue.

She got up and dragged a suitcase to the pallet and opened it on at least five thousand loose pills.

"What are they?" I combed my fingers through them. It would take several college freshmen good with their *PDR*s several days to key this load out.

"Berry good," my good nurse said, and picked one for me and placed it on my tongue. Where had I been all my life? How had I not been on a Chihuahua quest until now? What had been wrong with me? Why had I even passively plodded along on the group hiking trails? Why had I listened to Park Rangers whom I *knew* to be pederasts? I had paid my bills and stopped at my stop signs, and it suddenly looked as if I need not have. I may have tied my Reeboks a little looser than my peers, but I had strode the mall all the same.

At this precise moment a ghostly face *did* appear in the window, scaring a very modest little spurt of something out of my behind. The face was as quickly gone.

"Who was that?"

"That was Zeus."

"Zeus? The real one?"

"There is more than one?"

"Well, no, I—"

"Zeus."

I took a deep breath and swallowed hard: okay, I was *through* with all this Ranger Rick paint-by-the-numbers living and Cartesian logic and conservation of this and that and paying for what you get and getting what you pay for and being careful what you ask for because you might get it and vengeance is the Lord's and however many commandments and one and one is two and a circle is perfect and this is unique or not but not somewhat unique and the other million and one ways of staging yourself to die as if you were in possession of a street map and a schedule of trains. Since you were finally not in possession of a map and a schedule, who is to say that Yoo-Hoo and pills and Zeus making a bed check on you and your brown nurse is not the True Way? "Just tell me what is wrong with that!" I yelled at the ceiling.

"Shhh!" My brown good trained professional friend got me another pill and delivered it and calmed me with her cooing and we slept the sleep of sheep.

———

I lived in a sea of varicolored pills and brown flesh and pasty faces peering in the window. Not all of them were Zeus. I was left in the day to . . . to do with it whatever I chose. No discussions of purpose or plan oppressed themselves into our simple time. María went to work and at night we did pills and whoopee. We had no problems because we had no conversation. That clearly is the major undoing of relationships. I advise heartily against blather. There must be minimal communications of course, but in the battle of the sexes, as in any war, the communiqués should be tactical, brief, and if possible in code. María and I managed a coded brevity that was exquisite. I loved her breasts, her smiles, and her Percodan, and she liked my fox-colored starchy hair and that I did not strut around in banty swagger, I think. In the mornings when the poor thing had to ride the bus to work, I sat in the town square having mango and strong coffee and dark brown unlabeled beer. I pondered the absence of the kinds of problems one would be pondering Stateside. I pondered even this absence gradually less and less until I pondered the immediate: a mango without a bar code and wax on it, a coffee more coffee than water, a beer without a team of circus horses and a baseball team attached to it. I decided to name my fifty-pound Chihuahua Trotsky, or Mr. Trotsky.

On the lam in Mexico after a preposterous dog I have occasion to think of how *sane* childhood is, even its extreme moments and venues, compared to what we make of adulthood. This is why we go around chanting mantras about the value of maturity. We could not go on without this constant hypnosis. Of course—and I am living proof—if you do undo the hypnosis and prove capable of handling it, as I did when I mounted up on Tod

McGillicuddy's noble blue trike with my carton of chocolate milk, They will bind you over for the nuthouse, where everyone has had a vision of childhood and loss of the garden.

—

Dirt floors, sandals, foot baths in gaudy plastic tub. No deodorant. High-quality tortillas at every house. Butter and salt and roll into a cigarette! Eat it! A pig wanders the village and everyone knows whose it is! If someone took it everyone would know who! The pig knows whose he is, and *who* he is! Very little garbage because it is all valuable! Ice in an icehouse, abundant if you ask for it! Fruity drinks ladled to you and drunk from the vendor's glass, which he hands you, you drink, you hand back! One glass the whole operation! Want new clothes? Find a stand, take off your old, put on the new on the roadside at the stand, and walk off! Get a hat! Buy an owl! Amulets, spice, dolls! Birds, yo-yos, sisters! Sun, dust, rain! Heat, wind, cool! Day, dusk, night! Living, breathing, dying! Drinking, fighting, screwing! Laughing, weeping, not saying a thing! Flies, spiders, ants! Fresh, stale, pickled! Taking a shit, feeling fine, delirious with fever! Happy! Sunglasses! Naturally losing weight! Happy!

—

Answers are to be found, when they are to be found, in the dirt. Questions of self-actualization would seem to be moot when you find yourself in Mexico in lazy pursuit of an improbable dog. There are no angels on our shoulders after a point in life, and I've reached mine. I eschew prescribed medication. I sometimes contemplate cotton candy. I can tie my shoes. I cannot sing or talk spontaneously anymore. I can hardly even lust on impulse, if *lust* may be verb intransitive, and the world is vulgar enough now, at least in the sense of crimes against English, that I do not see why it may not be verb intransitive.

The beauty of mountain living continues unapace. I do nothing and nothing does not strike back. I tidy the house of an odd morning, though with the dirt floor the operation is one of judgment. You want the broom marks either all in one direction or describing a pleasant and regular pattern; the two cups together here, the two plates there, or a cup on a plate and a cup on a plate, as you prefer. The crow in the window is not to be teased with a shiny object. A gecko on the hearth is to be steered around: he will eat his translucent weight in flies. Then a coffee and a pill of choice about mid-morning, about the time you'd sit down and watch a rerun of *Lucy* in the States. I continue to fret the non-abandonment of Mrs. M.

The people here are friendly, whether dead or alive, mortal or god. The switchblade boys appear to have been an aberration, mostly. I do sometimes long for the odd breakfast cereal, but this passes with a good eye-to-eye with the crow.

I more and more display a contemplative nature, except that little in me inclines to elevated matters. Of occasion I take exquisite pleasure in a good tooth brushing and face scrubbing with a marvelous soap that they make themselves somehow from hogs and that smells of oranges. Grooming seems important when you walk about on your twenty-thousand-mile sandals. I am going to go soon in search of the fifty-pound Chihuahua, and I want to look good. If I am to be laughed at, I prefer an impeccable countenance. There is comfort in being deemed a *neat* lunatic. And less vainly there is the matter of being thought well of by the fifty-pound Chihuahua should one be found. One does not ordinarily credit dogs with discriminating in the matter of the master's dress, but this will not be an ordinary dog.

One day I washed my face well and got on the bus to go and find him. I felt very secure in myself. I did not care what happened. That is how everyone should feel every day, but in my case I need the artifice of looking for something that should not exist and, should it, that will make people laugh at or run from to feel "normal." As I grasp the nuances and vagaries of psychological disorders from my early brushes with the science, there is not much wrong with me.

—

In Chihuahua I found plenty plenary kennel. I found dogs the size of country rats with eyes the size of shooter marbles, with tiny, heavy-nailed feet that clicked on tile. I smiled at all these dogs and asked the breeders, *"Más grande?"* I have no idea if this locution was correct. It seemed that it was taken to mean something more like "More greater numbers?"—i.e., more dogs?— because I was invariably shown more (small) dogs.

It was my first day away from the house in some

time, and my feet hurt, and I couldn't tell if I was being
regarded unfavorably because I wasn't buying any of the
hundreds of dogs I was shown or for less obvious reasons; these people in Chihuahua seemed alive and
maybe I was back in the realm of common human inde-
cencies, the dogs made me nervous in ways I was certain
a big one would not; it got dark and I got tireder and lost,
black-cave-nightmare lost on a trail on a hill that may not
have been a trail and may have been not a hill but a full-
blown mountain. Things got black and steep and I
missed my María and the cool sheets and warm cinnamon and good cheer of a woman congratulating you for
doing nothing beyond being there. I began most naturally howling like a wolf. By "most naturally" I mean it—
these noises issued from me without a lot of thought. I
did not say, Okay, we are in extremis, estranged from our
friendly dead village, thing to do here is act like wolf—I
just started rather groaning about my feet and María and
the dark and then I began kind of singing the moaning
and then I thought I was sounding like a wolf but don't
really know what they sound like, but even that idea—
maybe I sounded like a bad idea of a wolf—did not occur and I kept at it, it felt right and meet so to do, amen.
And out of the darkness walked unto me, looking terribly uncomfortable yet happy to see me, as might be said
of any dog under circumstances like these, a forty-seven-
pound Chihuahua, though its weight I did not determine then, I simply knew it was close enough. It was my
dog. I had not believed in my lunatic quest until I saw its
object before me in hesitant devotion.

Already it was surrendered to me, leader of our

two-dog pack, and my self-esteem, which comes and goes, came. A fifty-pound Chihuahua, a mythical dog, surely a holy dog that I sensed was as old as the Aztec-Mayan mess I knew nothing about, was addressing me as Master on a lost mountain in Mexico. I shut up and said, "Home, boy," and wanted to name him but only odd names arose—Algernon, Cremator, Dungeonballs, Turk (not bad—he looked Ottoman), Oldsmobile, Tampax, Terwilliger, Tweezer, Toulouse, I got stuck in the Ts until I hit Trotsky, perfect, and remembered I'd decided to name him that, and Trotsky led us home.

There we were put to bed like a couple of boys. María wagged a finger at me and said *"Muy grande!"* to either me or the dog and put him on a pallet in the kitchen, where he stayed, and we went to bed as usual, fond and hot. She smelled great and was firm and heavy, I should say solid, "heavy" misreads but should be taken favorably. María is the forty-seven-pound Chihuahua of women. I was to have been the hundred-and-forty-seven-pound eunuch of Taco Charley's. My dog is the forty-seven-pound Chihuahua of Chihuahua. My head is a blunt instrument, a blunt instrument, and I don't care. María is a good person.

—

A good person is a can of worms. A can of worms is a ball of wax. *Sexually* speaking. No. I do not mean that. I do not mean anything. If that were possible. I submit it is not. One may not mean nothing, never. One may amount to nothing, "be" nothing, and nothing may exist in a philosophical sense, but one may never *mean* nothing. This is, I think, obvious: What do you mean? Nothing. Oh?

So I mean something. A good person *is* a can of worms. That is what I mean. I am not good, probably. But the measure, the measuring, is . . . well, a can of worms, I believe is the expression. The expression seems almost universally applicable. Even a can of worms is a can of worms. Everything, however, is not a fly in the ointment or a wrench in the works. Shoe polish is not either of these, but shoe polish is a can of worms, clearly. Shoes themselves, wearing them, not, securing the proper size, the proper support, *tying* them—just what about shoes is not a can of worms? Nothing is not a can of worms. QED.

I took to taking the long, regular walk with my short, irregular dog. We went everywhere and nowhere together.

Perhaps a word about my past is in order. I have one. As they go, it is not astounding, probably, or outstanding, certainly, I would think. But as soon as I make such a claim, or claims, I wonder what I mean. You know about the episode involving Mrs. M. and Tod's trike and my halfway-house time I have rather avoided. My presentation of these facts has not been altogether linear, I admit. I have said Mrs. M. is in indiscreet pursuit of me, and that that pursuit I have rebuffed. Something of the opposite might be the case. Or let us put it this way: I confess I was winder-peekin' before I rode away from the window on Tod's trike. That much I allow. Winder-peekin' is as old a crime and harmless as they come, and in my book if you have the urge to winder-peek you'd best go ahead and winder-peek. The suppression of this impulse can bottle up into a nuclear mushroom of desire if you do not just go ahead and do it.

But my entire life, this is what I want to say, has not consisted of winder-peekin'. It has consisted in other enterprise. I have had jobs, good and bad, mostly the latter, mostly indoors, mostly involving paper more than people, and I have pension funds in place, etc. Much like anyone else, except those folk in lesser-developed countries where trades are still well thought of and you can be, for example, a fisherman for a living without having to join the Ku Klux Klan. I have observed Christmas at the appropriate time. I have browsed racks of greeting cards and been unable to bring myself to select one idiocy over the others. In many ways, I am approximately exactly like everyone else in the human predicament. But lately I am not: not everyone is walking the hills of Mexico unchallenged with a giant Chihuahua at his side for protection and a giant-hearted woman in his (her) bed at night for balm. I have seen my dog eat cacti, how tough he is—flowers skins needles and that ornery fiberglassy down that *really* hurts, much more than the needles outright. He gives, I suppose, a cactus-eating aura and nobody messes with a cactus-eating aura, off a forty-seven-pound Chihuahua or off a mouse. I bask in this aura, drinking the occasional Yoo-Hoo, making the occasional sketch of hillside, whistling the occasional tune, inspecting the shoes I occasionally notice on my feet, the twenty-thousand-mile sandals, wearing well in the unpaved desert. My life, you might say, lacks definition. I *had* definition looking in Mrs. M.'s window, riding Tod's trike, drinking that chocolate milk.

———

Yes, so I have, as any modern burgher citizen denizen fool census-mark does, annuities and a litter of wives and lesser mistakes in my wake. But something distinguishes me from those doing their time, workaday halfway-house cons who do not take inspiration from a black cabdriver's insolence and flee country of origin. Let's just not go into it. I have made some phone calls and effected a cleaner getaway than it might have looked. There are realtors in red jackets showing my house. My modest man fired from Merrill Lynch for not pushing company stock on me is now holding my holdings at Smith Barney and observing my "conservative" investor-profile status, all interest and dividends on auto-rollover mode until such time as I need cash down here, which does not seem to be imminent. María does not know of course that I could buy us anything at all, and I find it agreeable not dwelling on it myself. I sometimes do wish I had Tod's Harley down here, but that would elicit more notice than is healthy. Halcyon as it is, there are still the switchblade boys in the hill and dale. My dog and I have done some naughty spelunking— unobservant of safety precaution, I suppose I mean—in old silver mines. These have a greasy groped feel to the walls that tells you the last thing you will *ever* locate within is silver, and this seems to excite us as to the possibilities of finding truer treasure. We don't know what, my bug-eyed hyper pal and I, but we look. Deep in a mine, too dark to see rock before you nose it, I can hear my dog pee from excitement in the soft guano. We squish on. This is life, perfectly put: go not you know where, except down, for reward already removed by those cleverer than you, sliding agreeably in ammoniac excrement, and "give up" and turn around with a sigh of resigned cheer with your boon companion, who does not complain. In Cincinnati, drink beer with grumbling colleagues until you all get DUIs going home to abuse the family. In untamed Mexico, drink a Yoo-Hoo with your dog and walk home and have a pill and a nurse. Altogether better way of life. Another thing: an egg down here is either in a nest, and usually not a formal one but one of convenience, such as a drawer, or it is in a pan acookin', or it is in someone's hand going to the pan. It is not in a box on a shelf in a store or on a truck going to the store or on a belt going to a box to go in a truck to go to the store to go on a shelf to go on a belt to go in a bag to go in a car to go in a house to go in a refrigerator to go from the box to go in a pan. I rest my case. Let your mind swell with the implications of the horseshit attending an egg in the United States and see how far you get. Gedouttahere is where you get.

—

I was allowed to work—the term is inaccurate: to get in the way—at the local *panadería,* and so was my dog. I hung out and flopped flour around, and punched it, and heaved it, and cut it, and kneaded and rolled and just generally had a sexy time of it. My dog was called Dusty. I contemplated his nature as he apparently contemplated me having relations with dough. He was allowed on the premises because it was believed he was the world's greatest ratter, but I do not think he is. At any rate, I have never seen him look for a rat or act like he

wants to locate one. It seems rather more correct to regard this dog as a gentleman, albeit a tense one who does
manifest a nervous eye toward my welfare. If I cough in
a cloud of flour, he edges up, prancing a little, to my side,
until the fit is over and he retires to a cool pool of flour
on the floor. If I slip in guano as we mine lost silver, and
whimper from the slick ammoniac turf, he licks my face.
He is a kind of bodyguard, but through no wit or will of
his own—people are generally terrified of a forty-seven-
pound Chihuahua.

I get off from the *panadería*—where, by the way,
no one fears Dusty because, as I get it, they are already
dead, and where I am accepted because once covered in
flour I am indistinguishable from the dead—I get off
and go home and make María breakfast against her day
abus. I feature the fried egg and the cigarette tortilla,
buttered and salted and rolled tightly. They've allowed
me a bag of *sopaipilla* from the *panadería* and these I
adulterate with things and put in a plastic bag for her.
She goes off brown and fresh and fed and coming home
to me. Wow. Legs! Kisses! No crap! Me and the dog and
my TV-free day! Silver mining with my dog. I am a puny
Tarzan with an apple-dome Cheetah and a robust Jane.
Jane is always robust, that is why she is Jane. Jane does
not say, "What did you do today, honey—nothing again?"
Jane says, "Estoy berry tire" and gets you in a headlock
and wrestles you to bed and buries her head in your unmanly chest.

———

Then the Revolution came by. That is all I know to
call it. It was a parade of men in Mercedeses, shouting

a formulaic something that contained the three or so Mexican names known to me before this my naturalization. It sounded like ZapatBoliTrotsGuevaraWhathefuckwrongwiyou!? I looked timid for a minute and looked to María for support and protection, a very bad move on the game board of machismo. But I noticed there was some kind of gentler current running through things; the apparent leader got out of the T-top through which he had been throwing the crowd epithets and candy and spoke conspiratorially with María, as near as I can tell about me. At any rate, they looked at me during this consultation, he at my head and she at my feet. I had the wit to go get my dog and two sugar scoops of the pills. I could not tell whether they wanted me for a ritual sacrifice or for some nobler symbolic purpose—a red-faced white man visible in the cause.

When I got back outside, things looked better and worse. El Revolucionario looked like he wanted to kiss María rather than execute or conscript me. The gang was impatiently revving the Mercedes Revolution motorcade. The entire scene had elements of a rabid young labor union, a Klan rally, a Hell's Angels mobilization, a football weekend, a fraternity rush party, a fistfight on a dance floor, fishing on a big party boat, and on the fringes a drug deal. That's where I stepped in: without any more ado I poured the pills from the sugar scoops into the cupped palms of all the revolutionaries. This raised my stock visibly and considerably. At the precise zenith of this coup of public relations my forty-seven-pound Chihuahua peed on a Mercedes tire. I felt we had together made a perfect declination to join the cause, either as casualty or as troop. And indeed the wet tire was noted with some chuckling and some pills were thrown back amid headshaking and the Parade of the People was off in half-circle blasts of dust and diesel and death to the oppressors. María and my dog and I stood there arm-in-arm, looking happily into the sunset. Is the cup half empty or full? I aim to get into my grave squarely and neatly and meet my private batch of worms without one more moment of horseshit intervening. Leave me alone—I shall dig my own hole. I do not recall being as centered, as easy on the feet of my being, since as a boy I took solid solace in keying out a snake or tree and playing a little ball. After that, things got pointless fast. And it seemed the job of everyone to accelerate the pointlessness and deepen one's commitment to it. This is where, if I am not mistaken, "failure" began to accrue: those who for whatever reasons did not or could not vigorously conspire in the proliferation of pointlessness began to "fail." The specifics of what I mean by "pointlessness"—oh, supply your own. Who cares. I've got a unique dog and a room full of no appliances broken or working and a woman not broken and no country that claims me and its revolutionaries will not kill me. Could I have more? I am allowed to muss myself in the bakery of the dead. I am allowed to prospect in old and lost mines. I am allowed to fall down therein in prodigious bat slime. I am *allowed.*

—

Many things are not allowed. People can have as many people as they wish, whether they can afford them or not, and consume as many cars as they wish, but they may not drive them as fast as they wish. This would reduce the number of people. And so forth. María and I had tequila *sopaipillas* following my brush with the Revolution, and got dizzy and bloated but otherwise felt very good. I saw more than the usual number of dead folk glance in our window while my tequila-*sopaipilla* buzz wore off, and waved at them all. I have not had, and not missed, *socks* since I've been south of the border. María slept nobly, flat on her back and breathing smoothly, which may be what attracted inordinate dead, after our biscuit buzz. It is possible my mother is in the hospital. No Son of Sam or anything, but my dog told me this, if in fact I have been "told" this at all. Told, "told"—it is not so suspicious: when you are told nothing—no phone, no mail, no Western Union, no pigeons—you find that you are nonetheless, necessarily, told *something*. This neat little fact is what, I suspect, really separates man from animals. Animals can do without, man must be told something. I doubt he can think one whit better, or has an ounce of soul or mind more, but he must be *told* something some of the time or he goes nuts. But a dog does not care if you keep the deepest secret on earth from him forever. You have never seen a dog longing for the news, and you never will. Yet somehow my world-stopper dog told me my mother, for whom I care not much, was hospitalized. I'm almost certain. He's forgotten it, of course.

———

One day the sky was albemarle. One day it struck me that the sky, which looked like pink and blue marble, should be called albemarle, and I left. Without telling anyone. I went back to my house, which was unharmed and did not look particularly vacant, and I wanted to go have a peek at Mrs. M. but she was not home, I could tell, and I wanted to see my mother, but I did not know where she lived. I took these impulses to be bad signs— wanting the unknown. An observer would hazard that I was regressing. I would not presume to know, but I nonetheless did feel—particularly in the matter of wanting to see my mother, whom I had no clue the whereabouts of and had not known and had not cared to know the whereabouts of for twenty years or so, but not so much in the matter of wanting to winder-peek Mrs. M., whose fiery red hair and supine openness constituted the kind of thing any rational sport might want to spy on if he could—I nonetheless did regard myself as displaying bad signs in some of this. Next you know I'd be turning myself in for my observational stay at Taco Charley's, which stay had probably compounded punitively in my AWOL into a term at the penitentiary, all for looking at a redhead and borrowing a boy's trike, and a couple of other things—I suppose there must have been something else. But I hardly see that a man in the modern world could be expected to play the role of a daily historian of his own or anybody else's activities, what with all that is going on and all the people and all the deficit this and riot that, and, well, the whole radio band of nonsense broadcast by everyone on earth of which it might be said there are even in a conservative reckoning about ten times more than we need, and I rue the day the Soviet Union collapsed and therewith the plausible threat, or promise, of annihilation of this 90 percent human excess we are suffering. I found some frozen bologna and bread and made myself a fried bologna sandwich with yellow mustard and ate it with a quaff of reconstituted powdered milk with a goodly stream of Hershey's in it, sitting on my porch watching for Mrs. M. and wondering why I was not in María's arms. She would be getting home about then and seeing my dog would know I would be coming back—a man does not abandon a fifty-pound Chihuahua. Or does he? I had suddenly to ask, looking at the facts of the case, where I was, after all, sitting. And the sky up here was merely blue.

—

I was held on what is called "72-hour mental hold." I was released on "personal recognizance." I was to report to the psychiatric hospital for a look-see. I got home and pondered my face in a mirror and decided that I did not recognize myself *personally* and was therefore not bound to observe the terms of my bail. I *had* no personal recognizance as I perhaps too narrowly or just too dumbly grasped the term: a bond had been put up for me by the court in good faith that it (my personally recognizing myself) existed, but it did not, and therefore they had no hold on me and I was free to "jump" bail, of which there was no actual collateral or security. So I did. As you know. And now back, inexplicably, I am very worse. I should not have left my dog, my grotesque dog I do not myself believe, but over whose leaving I feel like weeping, as if I were nine and the thing had been run over, is not merely "waiting" for me in "old Mehico."

"Why" "am" "I" "doing" "these" "quotation" "marks"? In all truth, comrades, I do not feel well. I am tempted to say "not myself," but it is precisely that amorphous— lovely word I do not know the meaning of—that amorphous not feeling oneself as I looked in the mirror for my personal recognition of my personal self that got me "fleeing" "the" "law" in the first place. I'm all amuddle. I sometimes have occasion, and this is one of them, to think about how extremely difficult it must be for homosexuals to pursue and secure the affection of their kind when it is so truly extremely difficult to pursue and secure the universally approved affection between heteros. Then again, I don't know of anything harder than your footprints being found under a Lucille Ball look-alike's window and you and your muddy feet being found on her son's tricycle, the getaway car. And you are actually charged with attempting to avoid arrest because of your use of a "vehicle." A Chaplinesque high-speed chase, and you to see real headshrinkers who do not possess the class to kill you before they begin the arduous process of diminishing your head. I once saw an ornithologist preserve a bird by stuffing its body cavity with cornmeal. Shouldn't that rot, or something, the meal itself, I mean, not the bird? I mean not the meal, the meal I mean not, I do not mean the meal. I become moxied on some pepper vodka and try to find my mother by calling city after city information, and think about giving up and turning myself in, except I am afraid to because I figure I will be charged with whatever unsolved serious crime has gone down here since I last saw my . . . my what? Who was I to have seen to establish . . . I am confused and will retire to write another day. I wonder what Roberto Duran could have done as a writer.

—

· *A Little Founders* and *The Iron Rescue*—these are titles that have come to me, whether from Mars to a part of my brain or from one part of my Martian brain to another. I'd be disingenuous if I did not tell you that I have just gotten out of a loony bin of considerable more swat than Taco Charley's. I have been to Chattahoochee without a banjo on my knee. Something happened to put me there which I do not remember, and most of what happened there I do not remember, but I do recall the later innings and the being polite and eating my Thorazine and the entire public-relations campaign you wage to get them to let you go. Convincing hawk-eyed authority whose job it is to find something wrong with you that there is nothing wrong with you is about like convincing people to vote for you for President—harder in the case of the loony campaign, because you are not heroic even when you win. You are at best, in AA parlance, a dry nut. A nut bar with the wrapper (temporarily) back on.

Mrs. M.'s house has a vacant look, and I fear I did something over that way which inspired this late incarceration and her apparent absence now. This is a shame, because not every man on earth, sane or no, has the opportunity to court a woman who is a dead ringer for Lucille Ball when Lucille Ball was looking good, which she was before she no longer looked like Lucille Ball when Lucille Ball was looking good. I trust it is apparent I am a man who knows more than the usual about desire, refined and not. Read my books if you doubt me. *The Iron Rescue* is light going but startling in its permanent truths. *A Little Founders* will break your heart, quite honestly. I am not all the way back. I am not coming all the way back. The bigger they are the harder they fall? Well, sir, the saner the deeper and more torturous the cave they chain your butt in, the more drooly your peers, the more of your daily boon companions you will see crabbing with kite string on the lawn or masturbating into the bowling-ball bag behind the nurse. The more likely you are to walk around like a penguin yourself, expressionless. Do not get too sane once they have their teeth in you. In sport, once hurt do not get too healthy. Fiduciarily, once broke do not recover too much, obviously prudent once bankruptcy obtains. Same thing here: a Chapter 11 of the mind. Stay down. I am. But like a turtle with a wormlike tongue, I can say an intriguing thing or two to fish.

—

This morning I am interested in vanillin. Or vanilla—it occurs to me I don't know the difference exactly. I am interested in that essence of bean that makes candy candy. That is all I am interested in. I am not interested, today, in Mrs. M. or straitjackets or Mexican lamming or improbable dogs, or in women or food or drink, or in newspapers or civil ways and means, or in jackshit. I am hot for a little brown bottle and a whiff of vanilla. Life as we know it in this late day of sophistication is predicated on the spectrum of one's interests; it is *judged*, to be more precise, by one's interests. If these are too narrow or too broad, or too shallow or too intense, we do not have a normal person. A man is supposed to be a kind of balanced diversified portfolio of modest interest in things, none of which is to get out of hand. A small percentage of his interest can be in high-risk matters provided the bulk of his interest is rock-solid conservative. Thus you see a man in a cammo suit on a computer-driven moving-target shooting range, shooting pop-up silhouettes of men with the aid of an infrared scope mounted on his very head, and bragging that he is thirty out of thirty, "About," he says, "what you'd have to be in a riot situation," and we have a goner—a white supremacist most likely—until it is revealed this is an assistant prosecutor with the Los Angeles District Attorney's office. This is a fully legal *hobby*, and my God, look at it, it looks like *exercise* to boot.

The sane have a balanced portfolio of interests, the insane have given themselves to imprudent investments—to high-risk, low-yield ventures. You do not look in windows. You buy lots of dinners for women if they are your interest. Take the newspaper; I sometimes think the newspaper was *invented* to serve as a benchmark for the sanity of man. You must take the paper and read it; you may even, if commerce is in any way involved, subscribe to and read several papers. But you must discard them promptly. The hoarding of newspaper leads to suspicion quickly. Fire marshals have a nose for them and a scorn for the hoarder nearly equal to that for the arsonist (whom they secretly admire, anyway). On the other hand, you may not *not* read the paper—this is uncivil.

Every venue in modern life is marked with a propriety of option similar to that attending the newspaper. The investor is expected to diversify, to be liquid, to mix one-tenth risk with nine-tenths conservatism. He deviates . . . well, he's deviant. Be interested in nothing you cannot sell—that is, be interested in nothing you cannot *not* be interested in. Here we get to the wicket. After dinner with her, take her home if she says to. A certain party will then go home himself; another will look in her window. QED.

QED my ass. Nothing has ever been proved. Perhaps in the old days—perhaps Columbus proved the earth round. Beyond a few rare instances of likesuch, what has been proved? What is *probative* today? As far as I am concerned the jury is still out—and a laughable concept that—on the entire modern world and all its doggerel affairs. My point. I like it when a person is moved to say to another, "Your point is well taken." This usually actually means "You are full of shit and I ought to kill you to get you out of my face but I do not see a way of doing that and getting away with it so I will say 'Your point is well taken' until such time as I can get an unwitnessed fatal blow in."

And things are heating up in my perception of the modern world: folk are stepping around each other in a more and more ritualized and more and more impatient dance, looking for the moment they can stop saying forever, Your point is well taken. In heaven it will never be uttered. In heaven you can say, Your point should be put where the moon don't shine. Right now I am smelling smoke and it is possible my house is on fire. It is possible this is my house I am in. Since Chattahoochee there has been uncertainty. I miss my dog, if I had a dog—I can't tell how far back this episode might go. I miss my dog whether I had one or not—there, a little assertiveness training to the rescue. But no one on the white-coated side of the fence would encourage you to lament the loss of an imaginary dog. My position on this, best kept to oneself, is that all dogs are imaginary. Is this Platonic? Can you pet an Idea? Can an Idea have fleas? Can an Idea kill the neighbor's chickens and get run over with feathers still in its mouth?

Stroke

[**A** woman comes at me armed with a weapon, her mouth, her clothes. The weapon is indistinct, mouth open, clothes off. Something is coming out of her mouth. It will hurt. The weapon is vague and bright— not nickel-plated, more accurate to say just nickel plating. It is bright essence of weapon, and not the true weapon. The true dark harm is in the mouth, the clothes removed. The *oglalasioux* jumble of syllables to slur on me, the jungle of hot flesh to be withdrawn once I'm listening, the platter of blind regret waltzing away with her victory. O dogs of solitude, lizards of horniness, we must prepare ourselves for Armageddon. If we only knew what that word meant. Islets of Langerhans is more like it. Prepare for that, boys. Call your mother and tell her flowers are on the way but she's seen the last of you and your practiced civility, you are going to the island. No man is an island is disputable. No woman is on it is not. I bid you adieu, Mr. Donne.

Then these dudes attack, with their women balled up at their sides. Then some more then. Now what?

This: Duwop Nura Buddy, a dog, was awalkin down the street singin duwah diddie diddie dum diddie day. I ignored him. I do not need a dog, let alone *another* dog.

I want to write a book sinful tradeout minnow (stroke) (related) (-) (stroke-related). A young man can have one. (Stroke.) Even so, he can still cross his *t*'s and dot his *i*'s, and cross his eyes (smile) unless they (antecedent: eyes, so you don't have to guess) are permanently crossed by the stroke. I cannot read my bank statements. Fortunately there is no money in the accounts or I would be in trouble. All life is trouble, degrees thereof. All flesh is sloughing, degrees thereof. All metal is rusting. All cheese going bad, or hard. All dogs leaving you, or refusing to. All women balling up into fists. All islands being washed by neaps and ebbs of loneliness. Not solitude, that is $100/hour loneliness, and islands do not pay $100/hour. Neap and ebb and spring, low and lower and lowest—who, my pretty, is the lowest tide of all? Out there run aground on the ebb, you can click together your red goody two-shoes until the cows come compounding interest.

I am silly. I am a quitter, also. These are the twin tines of the actual devil's fork. These days you cannot find well-made toys unless you are prepared to spend a fortune, a fact or surmise or opining that I tender in irrelevant position to my argument about silliness and quitting. On silliness and quitting: you can induce any roomful of folk you collect to volunteer by show of raised hands who among them has beat his child, gone queer, voted Republican, voted Democrat, voted Communist, slept with his daughter, laughed at Jerry Lewis, gambled away the trailer payment, flushed the puppies down the toilet, financed many abortions, coveted whatever, humped whatever, killed whomever, and denied it all, but not one of them will confess to being silly and not one of them will admit to being a quitter. *I slept with my daughter and I did not stop!* This reminds me of a joke I cannot remember.

I understand that songbirds are doing well in the nozoney modern world. In the vast expanse of survivors' electronic vigor and bitchamp, it will be prettily sung tunes and Hallmark cards and no one quitting, no one silly. The world will want a blacksmith. Mark me on this. Red wagon.

I met a woman riding by in a convertible, she looked sadly happy, I left her alone, you know, since she wasn't happily sad, a condition I might not worsen, sadly happy I leave alone—just waved to her there in that Fury III, wondering where she got such a car. It was army duck green; she had orange lipstick, oddly attractive. I saw a woman in a black Ford pickup looking neither sad nor happy. I saw a good saddle shop. I saw a turtle a time or two. I saw kites and hate. I saw obscene rain. I saw, I saw, I saw: *vidi, vidi, vidi*. That Caesar was a card. He had a tough but variegated line whore. Skip that (whore). I'd be all right if something would go ahead and happen.

Altogether, bye. Life is kapok, a material I do not understand. Lillie Langtry is coming over in her red Maserati, going very fast, to take me to lunch, because her husband, who flies planes on secret missions for the Air Force, is flying a plane on a secret mission for the Air

Force, and Lillie is lonely and so am I. That I, too, am lonely I have accidentally tendered as part of the reason Lillie is Maserati-ing over fast and lonely herself, but it is not, of course, my loneliness, that's part of her motivation. My loneliness, we should say, my horniness, is just happy-accidentally congruent to Lillie's loneliness, should say horniness. Captain Barfheart in the plane has the unhappily incongruent horniness, but he has all that ordnance and hardware and thrust and fire and speed to compensate, for the nonce, and all I've got is me bed, which don't fly and don't fly over Europe looking for red menace or over Libya or Iraq looking for sandy menace or lines of death in the sand. And silliness: he who will *never* admit to quitting will confess, once in a while, that he did a certain and specific silly thing in an *uncharacteristic* moment. But you can get him to admit he has slept with his mother before you can get him to admit he is silly. He ain't silly, and he don't quit. This is why I like the idea of Lillie Langtry coming over. Captain Barfheart ain't silly and don't quit—ergo thatair F-16—and Lillie Langtry going to kiss me, which is silly, and she going to keep kissing me till Captain Barfheart come home, when we going to *quit.* And I will have been silly and I will be a quitter. I am not going to say, Now, Lillie, you run off with me, we can outrun Captain Barfheart and the Air Force and napalm. I am going to say, Lillie, wash your ass and go home, and Lillie, also silly and a quitter, will. Red bird outside, blue bird outside, yellow bird in a cage.

I had me a four-pound canary, I could stop the world. No need to go to Mexico and find pills, either. I could just bust out of here and make it to Pets Aplenty before the pills I already have run out. They got more pills and Dixie cups in here than Las Vegas got dice and cups. Hmm, hmm, than liver got iron. Hmm, hmm, than water got wet. Hmm, hmm, than Howdy Doody got freckles—no, doodoo. It is a pleasure for an adult to say *doodoo*. I could just spray-paint me a owl. I believe they have a owl what is yellow anyway; I could just say it is a canary. Here is a canary. I am pretty sure he will eat yours. If your canary is lonely, put him in there with mine, I am pretty sure he won't be lonely after that. You silly son of a bitch. Cease pining for your Tweety-bird posthaste.

Why I'm *in* here, all this untethered *aggression*. Wanting a owl canary. Like wanting a dog lion. A minnow killer whale. Put your mouse on that ice cube in the aquarium and my minnow will knock him off it and we can see if your mouse can swim, then let's jerk off, okay?

Life is ash. I prefer a cloudy day early in the week, a sunny day late. Lillie has a fine smooth adulterated ass, heart-shaped and firm and edible like a Carvel cake. If Captain Barfheart called in a air strike, strafed the primitive village of my bedroom, it would be all right, provided Lillie and I were done. I'd have a calm moment there, still flushed with the testosterone ground fire, to think, I did not get anything I did not deserve. This would mean, neatly, and unusually—because usually something don't mean two things at once unless it's idiotic or, worse, cute (deliberately ambiguous)—that I deserved the bombing and that I deserved Lillie. A good piece of ass gets you blown well to pieces, and just what is wrong with that? What is subject to the appellate process, due or no, about that? If more folk would take a deep breath and take their being blown to hell, it would be a better place. Instead, it's: I don't quit, am not silly, and will not die. Someone *else* will be silly, quit, and die before I do. What would be funny would be if everybody had a statistician clocking him and posting his win-lose ratios on him, like LED tattoos. Marriage: 3–2. Child-support payments: 437–23. Get-rich-quick schemes: 0–6. Ideas: 2–567. Cars: 1–34. Sexual impulses to fruition: 6,784–21. Fruition to friendship: 18–3. Friendship: 0–3. Jobs resigned/fired: 8–13. Overall life slugging average: .183.

The ramparts about the Silly Castle would begin to crumble quickly. Life is sidewalk. Sidewalk is more crack than walk. All walk is side walk. Wabash, Wabash cannonball, downtown to the soul-food mall, not chitterlings but Nikes.

———

Decembre LX7, or sometime. I had a conversation with a mid-level Brit. I understand that is a coarse, if not crude, way of putting it, that they can place themselves to the millimeter in the graduated social cylinder in which they teem by hearing a sentence or two. I can deduce Not the Prince and Not a Cockney, leaving a vast middle ground where I don't know if my man went to public versus private, etc. Anyway, had one of these fellows, he took some umbrage or another, and I found myself "informing" him of "my position" in this fine, hair-splitting disquisition which suggested I wasn't a colonist but one of the true Empire cross, like himself, and this surprised him about as much as it did me. Unfortunately, or not, I have forgotten the speech and its concerns entire, and tell it now only because I know nothing else to tell. Life is lull. Life is many things other than personal-aggrandizement options and clear thinking about them. This is why people start getting excited at the prospect of hurricanes and kamikaze and death camps and bank robberies and such.

I know a man who is dying, and I should call him up. What stops me, for the moment, is knowing it will come to saying, "Jerry, I know that you are dying and I thought I should call you up." Actually, it will come of course to *not* saying that, when it is perfectly obvious to both of us that that is what is being said, and there we will be, in a Final Moment, lying. I will be lying to a dying man, a dying man will be lying to me, and we will feel worse than if I had not called at all. One fewer call, two fewer lies, humankind soars into the side of the barn. I do not understand, or expect anyone else to, that last little conceit. We fly gracefully, tactfully, a few minutes more, but into the wall of hick domesticity, even as one of us *dies*. Mayhaps I meant that. I know a girl named Tina who has thick ankles, but they support sturdy legs. She shaves these, and runs with these, and accuses men of sexually harassing her. I suspect they are not guilty. I know another woman who holds the same job Tina once did who has slender ankles supporting perfect legs, on which she does not, to my knowledge, run. She does not accuse men of sexually harassing her. I suspect they are guilty.

I suspect I am guilty. Of what is vague, so what I'd like to do is confess to everything, serve my time, and come out clean and debtless to Society. Just go in for about, oh, thirty years, read some books and be buggered, try to stay in shape, and come out clean-slated. Until, I suppose, you talked to someone, you would not be guilty of anything. You could be very careful about what you did, what you acquired, whom you promised what, and maybe you could remain innocent in a way you really had no chance to as a child, coming out of that prison. You would be in a position to tell the world where to get off the bus. I remember seeing Tom Snyder say to Charles Manson, "Charles, get off the space shuttle." This was in response to Charles's affecting to not know about the murders, which piqued Tom. Charles is in a position to say, Get off the space shuttle to the world. Next to Hitler he is the Hamburglar. But.

Life is dominoes and regret. That is the common view, except you are supposed to manage the regret to its extinction. Some buffalo near here were corraled for a brucellosis check and one of them was positive but half the herd died fighting in the corral. That is how you manage something to extinction. I've had trouble in my day with dominoes and regret—you can control more in life than you do in a board game or a card game, and whatever regret obtains isn't going to conveniently kill itself off in your lifetime. Regret is as perdurable as tar.

—

My back is stiff. Is that true, not true, relevant, not, sufficient, in-, necessary, un-? Life is cartilaginous approximating and infrequent bone-hard acting. Colorful tops that spin, children should, plenty of, have. Life I am not up to. It gets me down, and you'd think that funny but it's not, it's true, germane or no. How can the only thing we're here to do—whether you understand it or not—strike you as unappealing or difficult or as something you'd rather not do? In a firestorm of mystery and event, you sit fixed on the plain of combat, repeating, "I'd rather not."

When I got back from Mexico, I did not know what century it was or what sex I was, but other than that was fine. I felt relaxed. Felt. The condition of feeling relaxed when you are not is coma, if the misapprehension is physical, and comatose or catatonic if the misapprehension is psychological.

I don't hopalong Cassidy. There's weather and there's change, of clothes, seasons, silver. And of weather. The weather is partly moldy. Mocher, moody, mooch, moreso.

Aliens of Affection

[**A**ll along the watchtower—which he had
never been on before and now that he was on it could
not imagine what it was, or what it looked like, or what
he looked like on the watchtower, other than the way he
usually looked—Mr. Albemarle patrolled. At each end
of his walk, or watch, or beat—he had no idea what you
called the path he trod until the fog suggested he turn
back and tread until the fog at the other end suggested
he turn back again—Mr. Albemarle crisply about-faced,
having seen and heard nothing. He was on the top of a
wall, as near as he could tell, which was one of several
walls, as near as he could tell, constituting a garrison or
fort or prison, or, as near as he could tell, someone's cor-
porate headquarters. Where or how the term "watchtower" had obtained and why, he did not know. He was
not on a tower, and if he watched anything it was that he
not step off the wall into the cool gauzy air and fall he
had no idea how far down onto he had no idea what. If
he was on a watchtower, he could only surmise there was

a moat, ideally with something dangerous in it, below. But he had no actual vision of anything, and no idea why he was on the watchtower, or whatever it was, no idea why he was walking it and no idea what he was watching for. He had an idea only about why the phrase "all along the watchtower" kept playing in his head: he'd heard it on the radio.

What he seemed to be doing, more than watching or towering or guarding, was modeling. He kept seeing himself stroll and turn in the fog on the wall as if he were on a runway, and he had multiple-angled views of himself, as if he were turning around before a tripartite mirror in a clothing store. There he was: some kind of guard (for what?) showing, mostly to himself, some clothes that looked strange on him, or not, that he would buy, or not, and have put in a bag, or not; he might wear them out of the store with his old clothes in a bag. That moment had given him a good feeling as a young man— wearing, as it were, virgin clothes fresh from the rack to the street, his old sodden worn duds in a lowly sack at his side. There were no pleasures, large or small, in his life now. He had mismanaged his affections.

All along the watchtower, then, in the fog, he watched, he supposed, for affection. That was the enemy. It was in the belly of a beautiful gift, companionship, which gift was always good to receive until this monster of happiness began to pour out of it and run amok and make him so happy that he betrayed it. Nothing so sweet as true affection could be trusted. True affection is too good to be true. It contains, perforce, disaffection. He walked his wall, all along the watchtower. The fog was lustrous and rising and a comfort. Mr. Albemarle pronounced, orated really, as though he were Hamlet, or some other rarefied speaker, which he was not, the following speech into the fog, aware that loud disputations of this sort surely violated the prescribed duties, whatever they were, of those who perambulate the watchtower:

My specialty is the mismanagement of affections. A cowboy of the heart, I head 'em up and move 'em out: lowing, bellowing, grunting, snorting emotions of slow stupid tenderness driven in mad droves to their end. All you need for this, in the way of equipment, is a good strong horse between your legs. I am a cowboy, or, as they say in Sweden, a cawboy. Caw.

Some sodiers showed up. "Hey! Cawboy!" they said, or one of them said. It was a sudden foggy profusion of boots and nylon webbing and weapon noise, all halt-who-goes-there, etc. Mr. Albemarle defended himself against soldiers by calling them, in his mind, sodiers. He defended himself against not ever having been one and the possible indictment of manhood that might constitute, and he defended himself against their potential menace now—as they halted him when he should have been halting them by the terms of his not clearly understood position all along the watchtower—by calling them, in his mind, sodiers. The sodiers said, "Hey, cawboy, you got any cigarettes?"

Mr. Albemarle did and shared them all around, and they were immediate fast friends, he and the sodiers.

"You sodiers are okay fine," he boldly said to them.

"We know it," they said, lifting their heavy steel helmets to reveal beautiful multicolored denim welder's caps on backwards on each of their heads. They all smiled, each revealing one missing central incisor, right or left. There were nine sodiers and Mr. Albemarle did not have time to get a count, how many right, how many left incisors missing. He had once considered dentistry as a sop to his mother's hopes for him. A dentist talked him out of it. "I clean *black gunk* out of people's mouths all day, son." That did it. The same dentist, it occurred to him now, had earlier talked him out of being a sodier. "All you do is say, You three guys, go behind that truck and shoot the enemy. What's there to learn in that?"

This was a sufficiently strong argument, with the black gunk looming as well, to talk young Mr. Albemarle out of enlisting in ROTC and getting educational benefits to allow him to go to dental school. The final straw was the dentist's asking him what he, the dentist, might do about his sagging breasts. His years slumped over patients, cleaning black gunk, on a short stool on wheels, had not maintained a firm tone in the dentist's pectoral muscles, and they indeed drooped, reminiscent of a budding girl's breasts. Mr. Albemarle, who was then eighteen and in fine shape himself and not called yet Mr. Albemarle, told the dentist to lift weights, but to his knowledge the dentist never took his advice.

"You sodiers have good shit, it looks," Mr. Albemarle said.

"We have very good shit," they said. They each searched themselves and gave to Mr. Albemarle a piece of gear. He received from them, all of them standing all along the watchtower and blowing exhales of white smoke into the white fog, a collapsing titanium mess cup with Teflon coating on it that was very sexy to the touch; a boot knife that was too sharp to put in your boot; an O.D. green tube of sunblock, a jungle hammock, with roof and mosquito netting, a pair of very fine, heavy socks (clean), a box of 9 mm shells, an athletic supporter, a flak vest, and a jammed M-16 rifle that the sodiers thought was easily fixable but for the life of all of them they could not fathom how.

Mr. Albemarle put on and strapped on all his new gear and passed around more cigarettes in a truly warm spirit. "Do you sodiers," he asked, "know anything about all along the watchtowering?"

"What do you mean?" they asked.

"Like, what I'm supposed to do."

The sodiers looked at Mr. Albemarle and briefly at each other. "You *doing* it, dude," one of them said, and the others agreed.

"All right, I can accept that," Mr. Albemarle said. "But there is a certain want of certainty regarding just *what* it is I'm doing."

"Well put," a sodier said.

"We are in a not dissimilar position ourselves," said another, to general nodding all along the watchtower.

"We worry it not," a third said.

"A constituent of the orders—"

"To not know—"

"Precisely what we are about."

"So we just, as men with balls and ordnance must, go about the business at hand, whatever it is."

"And we suggest you do, too."

This made fine sense to Mr. Albemarle. "One more question of you fine fellows, then," he said. "Down there"—he pointed down and over the edge of the wall—"any idea what's down there?"

"Moat," a sodier said, "with something dangerous in it."

"That's what I thought," Mr. Albemarle said. "Any idea what?"

"Crocodiles."

"I think badly deteriorated scrap metal, like thousands of bicycles, cut you to ribbons."

"Get tetanus before you hit the water."

"Definitely."

"Get a booster, dude, you plan on swimming in that moat."

"I don't *plan* on swimming in that moat," Mr. Albemarle said. At this the sodiers laughed solidly and loudly, approving of Mr. Albemarle's prudence.

They all shook hands, and Mr. Albemarle thanked them for the gifts, and they him for the smokes, and the sodiers decamped. Mr. Albemarle was feeling good. It had been a fine rendezvous all along the watchtower, and as he resumed his pointless patrol, he patted and slapped all his fine new gear, more ready now than ever before for whatever it was he was ready for.

"I prefer the cloudy day to the sunny day," he announced toward the moat, trying to detect from any echo if it was crocodiles or bicycles down there, or anything at all. No sound came back.

—

Some aliens showed up. This was clear, immediately, to Mr. Albemarle. That they were aliens made sudden eminent sense of his theretofore murky task. He had been all along the watchtower watching for aliens. No one could have specified this without appearing to be crazy. Mr. Albemarle understood everything, or nearly everything, now.

The aliens were very forthcoming. They looked perfectly alien, no bones about it. All gooshy and weird, etc. They made calming hand gestures, inducing Mr. Albemarle not to raise his jammed M-16 in their direction. They slid up to him as if on dollies and said, "We are aliens. We are aliens of affection."

"What?"

"We are the secret agents, as it were, in cases of alienation of affection."

Mr. Albemarle said, "You mean, when a man finds his wife naked on another man's sailboat and he sues the yachtsman for alienation of affection—"

"Yes. We are in attendance."

"We are on that boat, usually," said another alien of affection.

The first alien slapped this second alien upside the head with a flipper-like arm. "We are *always* on that boat."

Mr. Albemarle offered the aliens of affection cigarettes and looked at them closely. In terms of gear, they were without. In terms of clothes, they were without, yet you would not, Mr. Albemarle considered, be inclined to regard them as naked. The slapped alien appeared ready to accept a cigarette until he received a stern look from the first alien and put his arms, or flippers, approximately where his pants pockets would have been had he had on any pants. Mr. Albemarle reflected upon— actually the thought was exceedingly brief, but trenchant—the apparent absence of genitalia on these aliens of affection. To his mind, affection and genitalia were closely bound up. The notion of secret agents of affection without genitals struck him as either ironic in the extreme or extremely fitting. He looked closely at the slapped alien, up and down, to see if there were misplaced genitals, if that would be the correct term. He saw none.

"What do aliens of affection do?" he asked, aware only after he did so that he might be forward in his asking.

"We alienate affection," the first alien said.

"There's Cupid and there's us," the second said. Mr. Albemarle expected him to receive another slap for this remark, which struck him as impertinent, or low in tone, but there was no objection shown by any of the other aliens. There were nine of them, as there had been nine sodiers. Mr. Albemarle was unable to detect the status of missing incisors because he could not determine, watching them speak, if they had teeth at all, or, really, mouths. They were weird, as he supposed was fitting. They were so weird that they weren't weird, because aliens are supposed to be weird, and they *were* weird so they *weren't* weird. He liked them, rather, but he was not as fond of them as he had been of the sodiers. They did not give him any gear, but beyond that they did not give him any comfort. Why should they? he thought. He had mismanaged his affections, and now it appeared feasible these guys might have had something to do with it. Every time he had broken a heart, or had his broken, maybe one of these gremlins had been there aiding and abetting, helping him fuck up. Perhaps this was the enemy. Perhaps these thalidomide-looking wizened things were why he was walking all along the watchtower in an ill-defined mission, preferring cloudy days to sunny.

"Let's take a reading on Loverboy here," the first alien said, and very quickly the slapped alien was very close to Mr. Albemarle. He had, in the popular expression, invaded Mr. Albemarle's air space, as had once a homosexual photographer who stood inches from him with wet lips and gleaming eyes and asked, "Do I make you nervous?" Nervous, Mr. Albemarle of course said no. Another time his air space had been invaded by a turkey in a barnyard, a big cock turkey, or whatever you called the male, which could in raising its feathers expand itself about 300 percent and make you pee in your pants if you were, as Mr. Albemarle was, disposed to be frightened of all things in a barnyard. Mr. Albemarle was not similarly afraid of a wild animal, but all things in a barnyard had been husbanded there by a human malfeasant who wore Wellies and had relations with the things in the barnyard, which consequently would bite you or kick you or step on you when they could.

The slapped alien stood next to Mr. Albemarle with

a gleam in his eye and had a lip-smacking expression, if a lip-smacking expression can be had by a party without, apparently, any lips. As he had with the photographer and the turkey, Mr. Albemarle held his ground, standing erect and turning ever so slightly askance to the alien so there would not be a clean, open shot to his private parts if it came to that.

It came to that. No sooner had he thought of that turkey the size of a tumbleweed in its waist-high dirty feathers gazing with its evil scaly wattled head at his crotch than the alien of affection touched him there very lightly and very quickly with a flipper. "Hey!" Mr. Albemarle said.

"Just a reading, old man," said the alien. "No fun intended."

"What's a reading?"

"We read your affinity for affection," the first alien said to Mr. Albemarle. Of the second alien he asked, "What's he look like?"

"Twisted."

Mr. Albemarle adjusted himself subtly in his pants and turned a little more askance from the alien who had touched him. "What do you mean, 'twisted'?"

"The worm of your passion," the first alien said, "is twisted."

"Well, it straightens out," Mr. Albemarle said.

"No," the alien said. "*You* straighten out, sir, as Johnny Carson once elicited from Mrs. Arnold Palmer that she straightens out Mr. Arnold Palmer's putter by kissing his balls. *You* straighten out, sir, but the worm of your passion is twisted."

"Your desire, in other words," the second alien said, now a respectful distance from him, "is not clean and open but dirty and veiled. Something untoward happened to you at a delicate moment in the opening of the petals of your heart—"

"Shut up," the first alien said. "Excuse him," he said to Mr. Albemarle. "He tends to make jokes when he should not. We are safer in not speaking of flowers. We are safer in speaking of worms. And the worm of your passion is twisted, bent, kinked, and not, as it should be, straight, straight, and straight."

"Is this bad?"

"It is bad, yes, but you are not alone. Only one person on earth we've checked out is straight. That's Pat Boone."

"Everybody else is . . . twisted?"

"More or less. You are more than less."

The second alien, who had taken the actual reading, said, "Lucky you're alive, man. It's like a Grand Prix course down there."

"What he means, sir," the first alien said, "is that before the engine of your desire crosses the finish line it must negotiate a tortuous course and use the transmission to preserve the brakes and discard and remount many new tires and—"

"Hey!" It was the second alien waving them over to the edge of the wall. All the other aliens were peering down.

"Can you guys see down there?" Mr. Albemarle asked. "Take a reading?"

The aliens of affection were whistling to themselves

in amazement. "Never seen the like of it." "That is bi*zarre*." "Takes the effing cake."

"What is it?"

"Nothing, man," one of them said.

"Nothing? Don't *nothing, man* me, sir. I patrol the watchtower and have every right to know what is down there."

The aliens went on marveling at whatever it was they could see or detect in the moat, if it was a moat. Mr. Albemarle looked in appeal to the first, apparently chief, alien, who pulled him aside.

"We've encountered the odd thing of the heart in our job," he told Mr. Albemarle.

"What's down there?" Mr. Albemarle observed the alien in apparent consideration of whether, and how, to tell him.

"I'm in *charge* here," Mr. Albemarle said. "Need to know." He'd always liked that phrase: we'll keep you on a need-to-know basis, so when they torture you, you will be on a need-to-be-beat basis for only so long.

"Broken hearts," the alien said.

"Sir?"

"About four million broken hearts down there—scrap hearts, badly deteriorated, cut you to ribbons before you hit the water."

"Not crocodiles or bicycles?"

At this the alien started laughing. The other aliens came over to see what was funny.

"What?" they said. The alien laughed even harder and refused to tell. They began goosing him with their flippers, trying to tickle it out of him, Mr. Albemarle supposed. Mr. Albemarle became embarrassed. He had said something, it was clear, ridiculous. But a moment ago, crocodiles on the one hand and bicycles on the other had made sense.

"I said crocodiles or bicycles," Mr. Albemarle told them. "I thought it was crocodiles down there, and some sodiers thought it was old bicycles."

The group of aliens politely tried to contain its mirth. The slapped alien generously came up to Mr. Albemarle and comforted him. "Understandable, man. No way you could know. We've never heard of it ourselves."

"I don't even know what I'm *doing* out here, all along the watchtower," Mr. Albemarle said. "Let alone what's in a goddamn moat I can't even see."

"Well, buddy," said the slapped alien, to whom Mr. Albemarle felt the most affinity (and he hoped it wasn't because this alien had touched lightly and quickly his crotch), "you know what you are doing now. You are watching over a giant spoilbank of broken hearts."

"My God. Still, what do I *do*?"

"Not sure on that. We break them. We are not concerned with their repair or storage. It would appear that these hearts here have been, in Navy parlance, mothballed. It appears you are simply to *watch* them."

"Watch all the broken hearts, all along the watchtower."

"Yes."

"In the world."

"Yes."

"And mine—it's broken, too?"

"The worm of your passion is twisted, sir. Your heart is up here on the watchtower, not altogether broken. We have no orders to break hearts. We merely alienate affection. The broken heart is, you might say, collateral damage."

"I have mismanaged my affections."

"That you have, sir. In spades. We have no orders to further alienate your affections. The reading we took of you was casual, informational only, whimsical."

"The worm of my passion is twisted?"

"Twisted badly, sir. But the worm is alive."

"Is that good?"

"Depends, sir, on your outlook. Are you an absolutist or a relativist, ideal or practical in your worldly posture?"

"I am a muddle of—"

"Muddlers, sir, do not go unpunished. The moat is filled with muddlers."

At this Mr. Albemarle peered over the edge of the wall, frightened and yet oddly buoyed up by this talk. He was a twisted muddler but not (yet) down there on the spoilbank of the broken. It gave him a sudden hankering to have his hair cut in a barbershop where they'd put sweet-smelling talc and tonic on his shaved neck and let him chew Juicy Fruit in the chair. He could chew fresh Juicy Fruit after the haircut, walking down the fair street with his perfumed head gleaming in the sun. He could find a girlfriend and try it again.

"Hey!" he said to the aliens. "If you guys . . . I mean, do you guys have any plans for me? Am I on the list?"

"No. You're singing the blues already, sir."

"Okay."

In a parade of salutes and waves—Mr. Albemarle did not want to shake hands with the flippers, and the aliens did not actually offer them—the aliens were gone.

—

When the sodiers and aliens had left him alone, patrolling all along the watchtower better informed of his mission and better equipped for it, Mr. Albemarle felt momentarily better. He had that new-haircut sweet air about him and felt he was wearing new clothes, and he stepped lightly and lively all along the watchtower.

But soon the drug put in him by the sodiers and the aliens wore off. The gear began to seem a rather *Sodier of Fortune* aggregation of pot metal and fish dye, and it was clanky and in the way. He discarded it in a neat pile.

What the aliens had given him was worse: the worm of his passion was twisted. This news, coupled with the revelations about the moat of hearts and about their having no call to further alienate his own affections, had calmed Mr. Albemarle when the penguinesque aliens of affection had been present. But now that they were gone he was nervous. It was like, he supposed, turning yourself over to the doctor during illness; you were still sick as a dog, but the mere presence of a man in charge of that in a lab coat and in an ethyl-alcohol atmosphere suggested your troubles would soon be over.

Now Mr. Albemarle realized the aliens had given him no such assurance. They had said, in fact, he was too alienated in his affections already for them to bother with alienating them further, which was not unlike being deemed terminal by the good doctor.

At first the aliens pronouncing "The worm of your passion is twisted" had had an oddly calming, if not outright narcotic, effect on Mr. Albemarle. *That explains everything!* was what he had thought. Now he thought it explained nothing, and where it had calmed him it frightened him. "The worm of my passion is twisted," he said to himself, and aloud over the moat, and all along the watchtower, feeling worse and worse and worse. "The worm of my passion is twisted."

Mr. Albemarle then had a vision of his genitals twisted into knots. This was oddly comforting, also. It did not bother him. He chuckled, in fact, at the idea, and he recalled a woman once at a cocktail party declaiming to people whom she thought interested but who were not, "My husband's genitals are like knotted rope." Everyone had left her and gone over to talk with her husband in sympathetic moods.

Mr. Albemarle knew that the aliens meant something deeper and worse, as they had told him, and that they were right. His passion was bent and his desire was dirty and veiled. He knew men whose passion was straightforward and whose desire was clean and open and who were not Pat Boone. They were true cowboys of the heart. They saw what they wanted (and knew it), they asked for it, and when they got it they sang praise around the campfire in a clear voice and got up early and made coffee for it and kissed it and hit the trail, the happy trail, until nightfall and bedfall and bliss. These cowboys had cowgirls: open-eyed girls in red skirts who danced with you if you asked and kissed you back if you waited long enough to kiss them first. And a true cowboy knew how to wait, and he knew whom to kiss in the first place.

Mr. Albemarle did not know whom to kiss because he wanted to kiss no one, really, and when he got tired of that he wanted to kiss everyone. At that point, waiting seemed contraindicated. Waiting for what? For *everyone* to say yes? It was ridiculous. He had the image of a real cowboy of the heart, his passion straight and clean and open, sitting a bull in the chute, packing his hand in the harness very carefully, and taking a long time while the bull snorted and farted and stomped and fumed and flared, giving the word when he was ready, and in a happy breeze of preparedness blasting into danger and waving for balance astride it for a regulation period and vaulting into the air and landing on two feet and walking proudly across the sand to receive his score, with which, good or bad, he would be content.

By contrast, Mr. Albemarle would not deign get on the bull until the last minute, and then would disdainfully sit sidesaddle on it, and it would erupt and the rest would be an ignominious confusion of injuries and clowns coming to his rescue. That is what "the worm of your passion is twisted" meant. It meant not a ride and a score but injury and clowns holding your hand.

Mr. Albemarle walked all along the watchtower, whistling gloomily and studying the clouds. He imagined the hearts in the moat—the aliens had said a spoilbank of hearts—in great cumulus piles, great billowy stacks of puffy, shifting, vaporous grief, under the still water.

He cupped his mouth and in a low, smooth, strong voice intoned to the moat:

"Cawboy to moat, cawboy to spoils of love—

"What am I going to do with myself, now that I know it to be useless? I am tenebrous, or tenebrious if you prefer, it's all the same. When the big bulldog get in trouble, puppy-dog britches will fit him fine."

The water, or whatever was actually down there, remained still.

—

On his next morning's patrol, which he went about naked, having liked the sensation of discarding all the sodiers' gear and not seeing the logical end to discarding things, he met a woman on the wall. This is the way it is in life, he reflected; when you go naked, for once, you run into somebody you might prefer not see you naked. There was a woman not fifty yards ahead and Mr. Albemarle at least had the gumption to keep going, not to run. His nakedness if anything emboldened his step, martialized it a bit, so that by the time he actually came up to her he was in a subdued goose step and was looking perfectly natural about it.

"Hey, *cawboy*," she said with a leer. "I been hearing you sing the blues up here all the livelong day." This testiness was coming out of an otherwise happy, innocent-looking woman reminiscent of Dale Evans. She had on the red skirt that Mr. Albemarle had pictured when he was taking inventory regarding straight desire and twisted desire. The red skirt flared out wide and short and had a modest but sexy fringe on it. It allowed you to see where the leg of the wearer began to be the butt of the wearer, and it gave the onlooker pause and a kind of stillborn gulp.

He was looking at this Dale Evans in her skirt saying this contradictory Mae West stuff to him, naked and in the arrested gulp and not now looking at the skirt or the legs or the legs grading into the butt, actually there was nothing gradual about it—

"Cawboy," Dale Mae was saying, "I want you to sing me some o' them blues."

"I don't sing," Mr. Albemarle said.

"Yesterday you sang:

> *When the big bulldog in trouble*
> *Puppy-dog britches fit him fine.*

You sang this in a clear campfire voice that lulled the cows and woke me up. I been sleepin' a long long long long long long time."

"That sounds like a long time," Mr. Albemarle said, stupidly, desperately trying to calculate how she heard him, where she was or had been to hear him singing to the moat. *In the moat?*

"Are you from the spoilbank of broken hearts?"

"The what?"

"The moat?"

"The what?"

"Is your heart broken?"

Dale Mae looked at him as if she had noticed for the first time he was naked, or as if he had lost his mind, which was, he considered, the same look. "Why don't you get dressed so we can dance," Dale Mae said. "Put on some of that *Soldier of Fortune* shit in a pile over there."

"Sodier *of Fortune*," Mr. Albemarle corrected, liking her. He fairly skipped over to the military paraphernalia and slapped on a quantity of it and stood almost breathless before Dale Mae in her flared red skirt and delicious fringe, ready to dance, or whatever.

"I warn you," he said. "I put you on notice right now. I have . . . The worm of my passion is twisted."

"It better be," Dale Mae said.

"By all assurance, it is *badly* twisted."

"When the big bulldog get in trouble, he should turn on some music and dance," Dale Mae said. "Take this bitch in hand, sir, and fret not your twisted passion."

"Yes, ma'am."

Mr. Albemarle did as he was told. All along the watchtower, they danced. It was a stepless but not beatless dance, hip to hip, pocket to bone, thrust to hollow. Gradually Dale Mae swatted away the annoying military hardware and left Mr. Albemarle as elegant as Fred Astaire, and gradually she herself softened and melted and fairly oozed into his arms, and they made in their heads plans to remain together and untwist Mr. Albemarle's passion and to do to Dale Mae's passion whatever in the way of no harm could yet be done to it. Dale Mae had a beauty mark on her cheek, which Mr. Albemarle admired until he touched it and it came off on his finger and appeared to be a piece of insect and he flicked it over the wall and thought no more of it and admired without impediment the dreamy, relaxed face of Dale

Mae, who had come to him unbidden and unhesitant and unheeding of certain dangers. This gave him a good feeling and made his puppy-dog britches fit him a little less fine. He was bulldog big enough already to kiss this cowgirl on the neck.

"Sugar," Dale Mae said, "it's the hardest thing to remember. All I can be is me, and all you can be is you."

"What's that mean?"

"I have no idea. Sing me some of them blues."

Mr. Albemarle sang:

> *What I like about roses I like a lot—*
> *I like a smell, a thorn, that jungle rot.*
> *I like a red, a yeller, a vulvate pink.*
> *And a king bee going down the drink.*

Mr. Albemarle and Dale Mae got themselves some coffee and got naked and got squared away for some intimate quality time together in a small bungalow he'd found in the fog, which intimate quality time Mr. Albemarle kicked off by announcing to Dale Mae, sitting cross-legged on the bed with her coffee steaming her breasts and looking to Mr. Albemarle some deliciously beautiful, perfectly joined in her parts and the parts appearing to be cream and vanilla and cinnamon and cherry and chocolate, and some of her looked like bread, also, smooth tender bread like host wafers—he tore himself away and said, "I warn you, I'm a bad piece of work, emotionally."

"Well, bully for you," Dale Mae said. "Do you know what to do *with me*?"

"I believe I do," Mr. Albemarle said, gently placing a knee on the bed and taking Dale Mae's coffee and setting it safely on a night table so she did not get burned in the clapping straits of his desire. He clapped onto her like an honest man. She returned everything he gave her by time and a half. It knocked him silly and made him pat his own butt, looking for his wallet, when it was over. He did this when he wasn't sure who he was. In the willing arms of an agreeable woman possessed of reason and courage, Mr. Albemarle had to doubt it could really be him she was holding and he wanted invariably at these moments to see his wallet.

"Relax, you piece of work," Dale Mae said.

"Okay."

He did. It was difficult, to do that. Relaxing was hard, and dangerous, he did not trust it. That was why you had drunks. They had the most difficulty relaxing. They wanted it most, feared it most, claimed it most, almost never managed it.

"I will break your heart," he said to Dale Mae, breathing hard on her breast, a sugary warm air coming from it as if it were a lobe of a radiator.

"Hmmm?" Dale Mae asked. "You go right ahead."

"Go ahead?"

"Why not? Break break break."

Someday, maybe today, he was going to do a woman right. Dale Mae's breast was next to his eye and looked like a cake with one of those high-speed-photo milk-drop crowns on it. He had a tear in his eye and was hungry for cake. It was *thanklessness* that plagued and dogged hard the heels of affection. Affection was that which, and the only thing on earth which, you should be eternally thankful for.

—

When Mr. Albemarle got up from these his exertions upon Dale Mae, the warm giving stranger, he felt fresh and sweet as a large piece of peppermint candy. He told Dale Mae this and she told him he'd better take a shower, then, and get over it. He kissed her and she kissed back and he took the shower and she was still there when he got out. Her heart hadn't been broken yet. It was progress. There was hope.

"It's not easy," Mr. Albemarle said later when they were strolling all along the watchtower hand in hand and in love, "to work this particular bit of magic."

"What particular bit of magic?" Dale Mae asked.

"Marriage."

"Indeed," Dale Mae said, noticing a piece of shale on the walk and throwing it over the edge. Mr. Albemarle waited to hear it land, curious he had never tried a sounding in the mysterious moat before. He was still keening his ear when Dale Mae said, "*This* particular bit of magic? You deem us *married*?"

"In a figure of—"

"In a figure of nothing. Not speech, not nothing."

"*Okay*. Sheesh! What's up your reconnaissance butt?"

"My what?"

"*Nothing.*"

He held her hand, petulantly but not unhappily. Marriage *was* a tricky bit of magic. Holding hands was a tricky bit of magic. She needn't be so hyper. There were—it occurred to him, now having been posted to the old verity that he was, whether holding hands or married or not, finally alone, always—there were people who had in their minds something called a "true marriage," as opposed, Mr. Albemarle supposed, to a *pro forma* marriage. He had no idea what this true marriage purported to be. He was not speaking of it when he constructed his pithy impertinence about magic and a marriage being made to work. He meant the false kind. It was a tricky bit of magic to *stay together*, was what he meant.

"I meant, it's a tricky bit of magic to *stay together*," he now said to Dale Mae, who squeezed his hand and patted their held hands with her free one as if to say, "You'll be all right." This little gesture proved his point: it was condescending enough that he wanted to take his hand back.

But she was, of course, right. Magic or not, tricky or not, it would bear no comment, it needed no more pressure upon it, the gratuitous happy union, than was naturally on it, the meeting and clinging together of two naturally repellent, irregular surfaces. They clung together out of desire but were aided, in his view, in their sticking together by a sap of hurt. This glue oozed from them despite themselves. For all Dale Mae's tough rightness, she was holding hands, too. She was very tough and very soft. She was nougat.

"You're a nougat," Mr. Albemarle said to her, announcing it at large all along the watchtower. Emboldened, he then said, a little less broadly, a little more conspiratorially, "True marriage schmoo schmarriage."

"What?"

"Schmoo schmarriage," he repeated.

Dale Mae thumped him on the nose and held him by the back of the neck with one hand and at the small of the back with the other and pulled hard with both hands, scaring him with her strength.

All along the watchtower, it was quiet. "I think songbirds are overrated," Mr. Albemarle offered. "Really inflated. Not nowhere *near* what they're cracked up to be."

—

Mr. Albemarle got them two buckets of range balls from a vending machine he'd never seen all along the watchtower before. As much as he had patrolled it, this caused him wonder. The machine itself was a wonder: a plastic fluorescent box dispensing not junk food or soda water but golf balls. What would come out of a vending machine next? Shoes? Pets? Beside the machine, incongruously to his mind, was a barrel full of clubs, for free use in ridding yourself of your buckets of balls. Mr. Albemarle got them each a driver, and he and Dale Mae slapped and topped and scuffed and hooked and sliced and shanked and chillied the balls into the moat of spoiled affection. Mr. Albemarle had the feeling that each ball contained a message of some sort to the brokenhearted from the not yet broken. They were like fortune cookies except that they were more like misfortune cookies. He could not imagine what one of these misfortunes might actually have said, and when he inspected a ball it read only "ProStaff" or "Titleist 4" or "The Golden

Bear." Yet he felt that each ball, whether it soared over or squibbed immediately down into the moat, carried a secret meaning from the players all along the watchtower to the wrecked players beneath it.

They had a good time. Each ball was a small celebration of their gratuitous, so far successful affection above the moat of moping: each ball said, "Here, you sad sacks, *here*." They were probably, in their hand-holding glee and innocent kissing mirth, only minutes away from hurling themselves like badly hit balls down into their broken brethren, but for the moment they felt fine and superior, lucky and happy, the way a new couple is supposed to feel.

Mr. Albemarle addressed each ball with a little wiggle of his butt and hands, a steadying sigh, *arm straight, head down, slow uptake, pause, how long will it be before she and I are back to normal, at each other instead of on,* whap! ball going God knows where, anywhere but straight. Mr. Albemarle could somehow induce a golf ball to wind up *behind* him. Dale Mae, in her red, fringed skirt, the fringes snapping like tiny whips when she cracked a ball into the ozone of ruined love before them, did better: her balls went forward.

That's how it is with women, Mr. Albemarle thought. They want forward, they get forward. Not so with me, which is where all the bluster obtains. *Talk* forward if you achieve backward. Bluster and cheer, the man's ticket to the prom. Bluster and cheer take reason and balls to the dance of life, and it goes reasonably well as long as the corsage is fresh. Then reason divorces cheer, and balls beat bluster, and the long diurnal haul to mildew of the heart is on. Mr. Albemarle teed up an X-out and hit it, smiling, best he could.

When they got back from the range, such as it was—the glowing ball dispenser, the ball baskets like Amazon brassieres, the clubs on the honor system—they prepared to frolic naked. Mr. Albemarle dropped his wallet on a chair beside the bed and out of the corner of his eye saw the wallet move. "Look," Dale Mae said, "there's a lizard."

There was a lizard coming out of Mr. Albemarle's wallet. It was nearly the color of the dollar bills from which it emerged, its head made quick birdlike assessments of the situation, and it ran.

"What *was* that?" Mr. Albemarle asked.

"That was Elvis," Dale Mae said, "in a green one-dollar cape. *Get in the bed.*"

Mr. Albemarle did as he was told.

———

There is much to be said for doing as one is told. Mr. Albemarle had come to see life as a parabola of sorts plotted over time against doing and not doing as one is told. Roughly, infancy and maturity were close to a base line of obeying what others expected of you, and puberty and its aftermath, which was a variable period, took you on the upward part of the bell-like curve away from the base line of doing what you were told. You soared on a roller-coaster hump of doing *not* what you were told and it felt good, but finally your stomach got a bit light and uneasy and you started, through natural forces and not reluctantly, to come back down toward agreeability.

Having ridden around with your hands off the bar and screaming, you were now willing—it was even exhilarating—to do precisely as you were told. It was fun in fact to subvert the voice telling you what to do a little by being instantly agreeable, by even anticipating instructions. This was pulling the wool on the bourgeois.

This was one reason Mr. Albemarle did not object to his current job, walking all along the watchtower. He still had no good idea what he was doing, despite the large assurances and hints supplied him by the aliens of affection, but he found doing it agreeable because he had apparently been, however mysteriously, told to do it. So he did it. Living well was not the best revenge; doing exactly what you are told is the best revenge. The blame or fault in your doing it, if any obtains, rests upon those telling you what to do. The masses of folk going over cliffs in the name of this or that religion were on to the beauty of this revenge, but Mr. Albemarle liked the less obvious vengeance of obeying the smallest whim, the fine print of commandments that were issuing like radio signals from everyone and everything around him, from the very fabric of civilized life. From utter strangers on the street to foreign governments, everyone had ideas about what you were supposed to do. Your job, as baseline parabola wire walker, was to divine their (sometimes tacit) wishes and appear to obey them. This is what civilized human life boiled down to.

Animals, Mr. Albemarle had noticed, and it was not surprising, were immune. They could not hear the radio. They heard only their "instincts," which excused all their nasty behavior. Periodically an animal would be

trained—i.e., forced—to listen to the radio. Animal train-
ers were, ironically, those most wont on earth to speak of
human freedom, iconoclasm, nonconformity as *summa
bona*. And they were, appropriately, dirtier than most
people, unruly, outspoken in hard-to-follow ways, united
beyond these traits in their insistence that tuning in a
horse or a bear or a dog to hear the radio of doing what
it was told somehow increased *its* freedom. These notions gave Mr. Albemarle the idea of opening an obedi-
ence school for dogs all along the watchtower. He would
train all the dogs all along the watchtower to leap into
the moat and become brokenhearted-man's best friend.
He liked this idea very much. Training a dog to leap into
space would be a test, probably, but it would be immi-
nently possible if you weren't soft-headed. The larger
problem with the idea was that he hadn't seen a dog in
all his days all along the watchtower.

When Dale Mae woke up, looking ravishing, he
said to her, "Do you think we need a dog?" She said, "I
don't think we *need* a dog."

That was that.

"I'm like one of those Iroquois steel workers," Mr.
Albemarle said. "I just naturally put one foot down in
front of the other, straight, without looking down, all
along the watchtower, whether there are dogs on it or
not, and all along the parabola of doing what I'm told. I
can walk that line as steady as Ricky Wallenda on a wire,
but no leapfrog."

"No leapfrog?"

"No leapfrog. Ricky Wallenda quit leapfrog. He fell
doing leapfrog."

"I see."

"Just do what you're told, but no leapfrog."

"I see."

The amazing thing about Dale Mae, about any tough woman who could still smile after enduring her own time on the parabola of doing and not doing as she was told, was that she *did* see. They could see right through a fog of nonsense to the rock or reef behind it. They'd abandoned radar in favor of a finger in the wind. This is why men liked them and were driven crazy by them. Men were content with a finger in the wind only when they were defeated or tired. Women used a finger in the wind cinching victory first thing in the morning. Without women, men would be giant raw quivering analytical anuses. Mr. Albemarle was comforted by this summation he had formulated and went to sleep on Dale Mae's bosom.

—

Mr. Albemarle found a writing desk all along the watchtower and stationery inside it so sat down to write a letter. "Take a letter," he said to himself, and by way of sexual harassment palmed his own butt and sat down.

> *Dear* [blank; he couldn't determine to whom to write],
>
>   *I know you think ill of me. That is because I am weak and mean. But keep in mind that* . . .
> [here he faltered] . . . *that* . . . [he could think of nothing now in his behalf, in his defense, to say to

the person or persons whom he could not think of either] . . .

Love,

Troy

Troy was not his name, nor did he want to assume it. He looked the letter over and liked it. It summed up his position nicely. It was all you could say if the worm of your passion was twisted, your affections were all mismanaged and *always would be.* "Keep in mind that . . . that . . ." that nothing. *Love, Troy.* Did he mean the city, the myth of epic war over an impossibly beautiful woman? Who cared.

He decided to make a thousand copies of the letter and somehow devise a mailing list that would be appropriate and have mailing labels applied by a machine so the entire affair would not be labor-intensive and he wouldn't have to lick a thousand stamps and write addresses and harass himself further. The sexual harassment of one's own self was the most insidious form of sexual harassment and there was to his knowledge no legal protection against it.

That want seemed a huge oversight on the part of the stewards of modern civilized life who had turned life into injury and redress, loss and litigation. The final moment in it all would be every citizen suing himself or herself for damages resulting from his or her own excesses and negligences with respect to himself or herself and his or her personal aggrandizement or lack thereof. The vista of the denizens of the modern world suing themselves into bankruptcy gave hope where there had not been any. This was a beautiful prospect to Mr. Albemarle, patrolling all along the watchtower—a kind of global legal self-immolation that would leave a few survivors who bore no one else and themselves no ill will. He suddenly felt, in possession of this vision, that he might be a prophet of some sort: the elect, here all along the watchtower not to guard a moat of the brokenhearted but to witness a Trojan War of Tortes. He was going to observe World War III, which was going to be a global litigious meltdown, from a safe purchase on his lawless wall.

—

Mr. Albemarle left the letter on top of the writing desk with instructions for its copying and mailing to one thousand appropriate parties, TBA. He had no idea whom the instructions were for, but if someone came along and assumed the duty it would be better than if someone didn't. Leaving the desk he noticed a phone booth he had never seen before and stepped in it and dialed a number.

"Hello?"

"Hello. Good, it's you."

"Who is this?"

"Troy Albemarle."

"Who?"

"I don't know. I just wanted to tell you that I'm lonely."

"You have the wrong number."

"No, I don't."

"You don't? You don't know me and I don't know you."

"You're a *woman*," Mr. Albemarle said, with more force than he intended, "and I just wanted to tell you that I'm lonely."

"Look, mister. That's what you tell your *own* woman, not a stranger."

"Look, yourself. If I tell my *own* woman I'm lonely, she'll think me silly."

"Maybe you are."

"Maybe I am. I don't dispute it. But to admit that one is silly is not to deny that one is lonely."

"It probably accounts for it."

"It *probably does!*" Mr. Albemarle all but shouted, slamming the phone into its chrome, spring-loaded cradle, fully satisfied.

When he saw Dale Mae approaching with a shotgun, he thought to test the wisdom of the conversation with the strange woman, with whom he was in love.

"Dale Mae, I'm lonely."

"Don't be silly," Dale Mae said.

"Yes!"

"What's the matter with you?"

"Nothing."

"Do you want to shoot some skeet?"

"Of course I want to shoot some skeet."

"Well, come on. There's a skeet range down the way."

"I never saw a *skeet range* all along the watchtower," Mr. Albemarle said. "A *lot* of things, actually, are—"

"Come on, lonely heart. My daddy taught me one thing and I'm going to show you what it is."

"Do, do, do," Mr. Albemarle said, taking a look around for the presence of witnesses to this exchange. There were none that he could see, which, he knew, meant not much. *Nothing apparent* meant more, in these days, than *something obvious*. He was getting used to that. It took some doing, but he was doing it.

The skeet range was of the nothing-apparent type. Dale Mae stopped walking, put two shells in her gun, and crisply closed it, looking dreamy-eyed at Mr. Albemarle and patting the gun and saying of it "Parker" in the lowest, sexiest voice he'd ever heard, and then her eyes cleared and she turned to face the void beyond the wall, said "Pull," and blew to infinitely small pieces a thing which seemed to fly from the front face of the wall. It looked like a 45 rpm record before she hit it; Mr. Albemarle concluded it had been a clay skeet after she hit it. She kept saying "Pull" and blasting that which flew, left right high low, to bits, and she took a long, lusty snort of the thick cordite smell in the air and scuffed some of the wadding from her shells off the wall and said, "Mone get me some iced tea and fried chicken when I get through shooting, and then kiss you to death," and resumed firing, shooting backwards and between her legs and one-handed from the hip, like a gunslinger with a three-foot-long pistol, *missing nothing*, and Mr. Albemarle started talking, uncontrollably, agreeably:

"In the first grade had a teach name Mrs. Campbell that was the end of sweetness for me in the, ah, official realm. Next year ozone, I mean second grade in orange groves, etc. Mother had water break and taxi to hospital, golf-course father, had swimming lessons chlorine nose.

A siege of masturbation ensued. Declined professional life—had *choice,* too. Somehow at juncture early in life where you elect to watch birds or not I deigned not. *Fuck birds.* This is sad. I am holy in my disregard of the holy. Sitting upright in a Studebaker or some other classically lined failure is the attitude in which I see myself for a final portrait in the yearbook of life. Depth charges *look* like 55-gallon drums, but I suspect they are really not that innocent-looking up close. Reservations at hotels and restaurants and airlines are for—" He stopped and snorted lustily the cordite himself and realized he had been aping Dale Mae's shooting in mime. He looked like a fool. She kept shooting. She was a one-person firefight. She would fill the moat with clay shards and wads.

"I want the certainty of uncertainty. I declare nothing to customs, ever. Transgressions of a social and moral sort interest me: philosophically, I mean. They assume— I mean those *who* assume to know a transgression—that points A and B for the gression to trans are known. I've had trouble, since the ozone of second grade and the chlorine and my mother holding herself, having peed in her pants and cursing my father, and since the large beautiful hognose snake I was too scared of to pick up in the orange grove so went home to get a jar to invite him to crawl into, which took about a half hour, and well, the snake didn't wait around, I've had trouble knowing point A and point B in order to correctly perceive, or conceive, transgression."

"Let's go get some chicken," Dale Mae said.

"That sounds delicious. That sounds good. That sounds not urbane but divine anyway—"

"Shut up, baby. I can't kiss you, you go off your rocker."

"You shoot that gun I shoot my mouth, is all. I—"

There was, not improbably, tea and fried chicken in a handsome woven basket, and a red-checkered table-cloth for them to have the picnic on, all along the watch-tower.

—

Selling hot, melted ice cream from a rolling cart, like soup, or to put on pastries, or something, he sup-posed, Mr. Albemarle pushed an umbrellaed cart all along the watchtower. It had four rather small wheels in-stead of the more conventional two large wheels used by food vendors, and they flibbered and squalled, drawing his attention away from trying to figure whose idea it was to try to sell hot ice cream to pondering how much of life, finally, was pushing things around on wheels. The sick were flibbering and squalling down halls of disinfec-tant, the healthy down freeways of octane, dessert in a good restaurant flibbered and squalled up to you in a cart much like his—if the human race had gone as mad for fire as it had for the wheel, the earth would be a black cinder. Instead, it was a scarred, run-over thing, tracks all over it, resembling in the long view one of the world's largest balls of twine, in this case one as large *as* the world.

Dale Mae was down the way and Mr. Albemarle moved along the way. Who was going to buy hot ice cream? Who, all along the watchtower, was going to buy anything? There *was* no one all along the watchtower, so far, except the sodiers, the aliens of affection, and now Dale Mae. Mr. Albemarle looked around to see if perchance anyone was watching and pushed the cart of bubbling ice cream—it smelled cloyingly sweet—over the edge of the watchtower into the moat, brushing his hands together briskly as if he'd handily completed a nasty task. He whistled a happy tune, one that appeared to be random notes, and sauntered all along the watchtower.

Mr. Albemarle stopped his whistling and sauntering in mid-blow and mid-step. He had an old-fashioned crisis. He was suddenly transfixed by one of the old human anti-verities: *he had no idea what he was doing, or was supposed to do*. Pal with sodiers, let aliens of affection feel you up, romp with a Dale Mae, push boiling ice cream into a moat—these things you did in life because they came along. You did them. You even did them well, if you cared to—Dale Mae said the worm of his passion was *exquisitely* twisted. But so what? What of it? What *then*? What *now*? What *point*?

He stood there feeling slump-shouldered and low. He had a vision of a different kind of life. There were men who, say, ran car dealerships and bought acreage and had their friends out to shoot quail and they all drank out of these Old-Fashioned glasses with pheasants painted on them, painted "by hand" it said in the expensive mail-order catalogue the car-dealer quail-shooter's wife ordered the glasses out of. The wife and the other wives were in the kitchen discussing what the wives of car dealers and bankers and brokers discuss. They were wearing pleated Bermuda shorts and none of them was too fat. The men were content with them, even loved them, and did not have affairs too much. The men laughed easily among themselves at things that were not too funny. Mr. Albemarle was outside this, all of this.

He knew that were he inside it, the point-of-life problem might not be resolved, but he knew it would not, if he were drinking Wild Turkey and talking Republican politics, come up. From his vantage and distance, quail glasses and okaying the deficit might well be *exactly* the point of life, he could not tell. But he was certain that he—all along the watchtower, with (accidentally) a woman who could (incidentally) shoot the quail but who would (certainly) shoot the quail glasses also—was never going to get the point. He was, he realized, standing there looking at the ball. He did not see that it helped anything. If you paused to look at the ball, you were going to be tackled for no gain, or for a loss; whereas if you just at least *ran*, you stood a chance of gaining yardage. That you had no idea what a yard meant was no argument to lose yardage, or was it? How had he gotten to walking all along the watchtower? Was it not a losing of yardage? Was being on the watchtower with a woman who could probably shoot the painted quail off a glass without breaking the glass not somehow the negative image of life on the plantation, where the plantation had nothing planted on it but feed for the birds who would be painted on the glasses lovingly held and admired as symbols of the good life? At this cerebration Mr. Albemarle was forced to sit down and say, "Whew!" He'd had, he thought, some kind of epiphany. "Whew!" he said again. It helped.

"What's wrong with you?" Dale Mae said, scaring him. He'd not heard her come up. He wondered if the watchtower was getting softer, or something.

"Nothing," he said. "If I threw a hand-painted quail glass in the air, could you shoot the paint off it without breaking the glass?"

"Do it all the time," Dale Mae said. "Problem is catching the glass. That's hard. Usually you get you a party of car dealers and brokers to shag 'em. Out there in their Filson pants and Barbour coats, pumping hell-for-leather through the gorse, flushing actual quail. There are ironies."

Mr. Albemarle looked at her hard. Either she was demonic and had possessed his brain or something else of a weird and too intimate nature was going on.

"Where are the wives?" he asked.

"What wives?"

"To the glass catchers."

"In the kitchen with Dinah strummin' on the old banjo."

"Thought so."

"Let's get us some ice cream."

"Can't."

"Why not?"

"I rolled the cart into the moat."

"You *what*?"

"Well, it was *boiled* ice cream. Did you want *boiled* ice cream?"

"No. I want hard cold ice cream."

"Me too."

Like that, they were together, hand in hand, strolling all along the watchtower looking for ice cream proper, Mr. Albemarle's epiphany behind him.

———

They walked by the writing desk where Mr. Albemarle had left instructions for the phantom secretary to mail his one thousand letters it seemed just seconds before, and the desk was covered in vines. He remarked on it to Dale Mae.

"Heart mildew," Dale Mae said.

"What's that?"

"It's what grows on sites of affection. If you'd left that desk alone, or left a real letter on it that was to be mailed to one thousand people for whom you never had or expected to have affection, there'd be no vine on it. Your letter, lame-o one that it is, brings on the jungle. Am I on that mailing list?"

"Not yet. I only have the brokenhearted on that list."

"A thousand?"

"Well, I rounded up."

"As well you might. As well might we all. It is a proposition of such close tolerances, at least before the parts are worn out from friction, that pairing a thousand bolts to a thousand nuts does not seem excessive. Consider thread count, mismatched metals—"

"Dale Mae, could we talk about something else?"

"Sure, baby. What?"

"I once threw away a Craftsman circular saw when all that was wrong with it was a broken tooth on a drive gear. This, the whole-thing throwing away, was a waste. I regret it. That whole saw—motor, blade, and all—in a plastic garbage bag, now in a landfill, I guess, with its bad gear nearby somewhere in the great noncomposting amalgam of jetsam, if you have jetsam on land, or flotsam, I don't know the difference, but anyway it, the saw, in its exploded view (I did not reassemble it) is packed into some clayey sand with whatever else I threw away with it and whatever else other people threw away that day, and there are seagulls flying overhead so maybe it's fair to call the saw flotsam, or jetsam, where you have gulls you have salvage, just as where you have smoke you have fire."

"Is that it?" Dale Mae asked.

"No. That is the tip of the lettuce. I once took four baby cardinals from their nest in a relocation program of my own devising. They, the hairless little blue pterodactyls, were to be moved to a 'safer' place, God knows where. For this transport they were placed on a wooden paddle of the sort you are to strike a rubber ball with repeatedly as it returns to the paddle via an elastic band. I have blocked the name of the toy."

"Fly Back," Dale Mae said.

"The birds," Mr. Albemarle said, "peeping and squalling, were red-skinned and blue-blooded underneath the fine cactusy down on them, giving them a purple scrotal texture until they fell off into an ant bed. The kind of squirming they did, which made me unable (afraid) to cup them on the paddle, did not look radically different from the kind of writhing they did once they fell off and the ants were on them, but it was. They writhed to death, the baby cardinals, right there at my feet, at the foot of the tree in which their erstwhile happy safe home sat empty but for the hysterical parents flitting in and out. Right there at my feet, except I slunk my feet off somewhere to contemplate what went wrong, how the little bastards should have known better than to *scare me* like that."

"Is that it?"

"No. Another time I sold a puppy to the right people and bought it back and sold it to the wrong people, who got it stolen. The right people I *thought* the wrong people were kids in a garage band who wanted the dog to protect their equipment. When I got there to buy back the puppy, it was on the knee of one of the boys, watching cartoons with them. *I took the dog back.* Then I resold it to a family man who had children not yet rock 'n' roll age. He managed to let the dog be stolen, which the rock 'n' roll boys would never have done. And what would protect the boys' amps and drums and guitars now? My point is that my entire life is probably just a series of this kind of blind self-serving fuckup. *Everything* is cardinal-nest robbing and taking puppies from watching cartoons with their devoted new masters. *Every breath is dumb.* Even if you are on to this, you have no way of proving it. But the principle of reasonable doubt obtains. There is reasonable doubt that I have done one sensible thing in my life."

"Is that it?"

"That's it."

"You need to chill."

"To what?"

"Chill."

"Are you black?"

"Do I look black?"

"My point is, let them have their baby cardinals. Don't put them on your paddle," Mr. Albemarle said.

"Oh, brother."

"Are we having a fight?"

"No, babe. We are going to bed. You're a case."

"Well, bully for me."

Dale Mae smelled of gun oil, and Mr. Albemarle kissed her recoil shoulder, imagining it slightly empurpled from her shooting, but it was not. Her shoulder was pale and strong. She cleared his head of broken saws and wheeling gulls and writhing blue baby birds and misplaced dogs.

He put all of what was left of his desire, dumb or twisted or not, on top of and in this Dale Mae, and went through the motions, which is to say, vulgarly, made *the* motion, the curious in-out yes-no which all primates figure out or they die out, and it was a more or less standard bedroll except that not only did Mr. Albemarle's astral body levitate above them but *two* astral bodies levitated above them, and impersonally looked at him doing this personal thing. This always happened with his one astral body, but with these his two astral bodies the impersonal viewing of his doing the personal thing, yessing noing yessing, was in stereo, as if he were a card in the trombone slide of a stereopticon.

As happens in that moment when the illusion of three dimensions obtains, Mr. Albemarle felt himself deepening, receding, *going in*. He lost himself in the picture a bit, or altogether, and lost himself in the personal thing, in the vulgar, in the sublime, in Dale Mae, in a hallowed and haunted way that 3-D pictures viewed this way can be hallowed and haunted, more rich-seeming than the flat life that their two separate views depict. He left his common dimensions. He got into it.

His mind decamped. He thought he saw the sodiers for a moment on his left, the aliens to his right, in tiered banks and waving at him as if he were on a float in a parade. He looked at Dale Mae but did not see her clearly—more precisely, he saw clearly *into her pores* if he saw clearly anything at all. The watchtower *was* getting softer, he thought, absurdly. The brick was turning to mush, his mind was turning to mush, he did not much mind. Had he been in the tiers of parade watchers waving, he would happily have waved at himself going by, or rather down, the street, or the tunnel, down whatever, wherever he was going, happily, down. He had waited a long time for once-was-lost-now-am-found, and he had no reservations about its general oddness or peculiar particulars. Dale Mae herself was already behind him, a warm soft old way of being. He was a new man, even if that meant, as it seemed to, not being exactly a man. That—exactness—was exactly what was being lost. It was being lost with an inexact agreeableness that felt at once intellectually irresponsible and shrewd. Mr. Albemarle was gone.

[*Dump*

[**W**ife, child gone, phone-tree confirmation, 1–800 FAM GONE. I shall eat this pork chop and wine. Breakfast of chop and wine, blue wine pink chop, sweep the floor, clean house. Dust-free environment in which to begin breathing. Down. Wine and chop. Chop. Wine. Purple.

I have some credit in the women bank, but not in the child bank. Never heard of the child bank. There is no solace for the lost child. There is solace for the lost woman. There are lost more women. You eat chop, call woman, sweep floor. Rooms full of bears and books cannot be swept. Remain in the public open spaces, sweeping light dust, not heavy artifacts, nothing so heavy as the stuffed animal just now. Leave them be. Maybe forever. Put on apron and sing. Someone's in the kitchen with Dinah, someone's in the kitchen, I know, ho, ho, and it's you.

REPENT
FINAL
WARNING

A road sign like this, invariably nailed to a *pine* tree, high and aslant, you never pay more heed to than it takes to chuckle.

WINE

FINAL

CHOP

I am in recovery. From what is not precisely known. From life, mostly, about covers it. *Everything* is dependence and abuse or denial of same. *Everything* is a cover for something. Booze covers for your boring, lack-of-inner-resource self (mothers accuse you of that lack, and you may hate your mother according to her being wrong or, usually, right, but mine never so accused, and I hate her anyway, or at least a girlfriend says I do, a girlfriend of whom I may not be altogether fond herself). Recovery from the "discovery" which every moment in your existence past about age five has been pointing to, but for which you had not properly sat the jury so managed not to notice, that you are an ass. I am in recovery from that revelation. My dung heart reels. I stupe. Ass wipes nose, has sniffles. Regroups. Wine, chop. Floor, clean. Dust. Sun. Phone. Who?

—

A clean room in a unlit place. A green breeze and salt. Time. Time ticking, grasshoppers. Dry-cured bacon and big-time blues. Mean to dance, mean to call a *girl*. Mean to affect the effect of getting my effects in order. Mean to dizz out.

I want a girl impervious to harm, petty or grand. An

industrial model disguised for home use. For the contractor masquerading as home owner.

—

A day at the dump to provide some distraction. I have come with Driggers to the dump. Driggers has been to the barbershop and smells like a woman and is as pretty and is very proud of his grooming and is smacking gum and doing okay until he reports, "Flashback."

"Flashback of what?" The way he's all pretty-boyed and dancing from goner appliance to reparable appliance, stopping to look at girlie magazines blowing in the flyblown breeze, I expect him to say, "Pussy."

He says, "Vietnam." He stands where he is with a truly vacant, sick look on his erstwhile smiling face. Much of life, for me, resides in moments in which you might not too absurdly use "erstwhile," but Driggers is not so idle or full of shit.

What around us—gales of seagulls preying on garbage, the predominate strains of which are these torn-up *Penthouses*, and inexplicable case lots of Skoal—could remind him of Vietnam?

"Vietnam? What the fuck out here is like Viet—"

"That bulldozer."

For the first time in my dodger life, I see the horror, the horror. The bulldozer is an anemic yellow in hot white light and diesel pestilence moving tons of waste with flies on it. I don't want to know more. This is frightening in a way that Tales of Charlie are not: or pungee sticks, or dried ears, or tunnels, or the saps who went being better than those what did not.

"We have to stop drinking, Driggers, but it doesn't have to be today. Let's go." He is in the truck, white.

It starts.

—

I want to love but know I never will. Or is it that I want to be loved and know that that, too, I can prevent? Or must prevent? I can locate the *object*, it is in the *method* I fall down. Do not quite have the hang of it. This is a difficult idea to get your brain on, in the truck with Driggers, who is calmed into an earthly earthy mania. You could not hold the idea in your head that you did not quite get the hang of, say, eating. On the face of it, the idea is absurd: who doesn't get eating? But once you look at it—bologna, Miracle Whip, tofu, "cheese food product," the diet industry, the *food* industry, for that matter—it is tenable that many people do not have the hang of eating. So how difficult the notion they do not know how to love? Simple idea, really. We are drunk and do not have the hang of drinking.

Driggers will get so drunk tonight I will have to prevent him from killing someone. Driggers has the hang of killing. He is now most agreeably sampling the tins of Skoal I pressed him to take. There were so many of them, with sales literature and still in case boxes, looking not only unopened but otherwise unharmed, that we know something is wrong with them. But short of cyanide injection—and why would a killer put his killer Skoal *in the dump*?—we can't figure what is wrong with them. Driggers is tentatively tasting multiple tins, sampling flavors he has never bought. He's getting happy. Comparatively. Tonight that 'dozer and that Nam will hover about the pool table, and I will have my work cut out for me. Those of us who did not go can yet be Good Boys.

Driggers and I matriculate smoothly from the dump to the bar, a good one about like the dump, no seagulls allowed. Actually a species of seagull is allowed. It sits at the bar from 11 a.m. on, and at about 7 p.m. starts flying from man to man. And at about 10 that night Driggers and I do the Act. He beats everybody in the place once on the pool table and circles around to the first boy he beat and says to him, "Rack 'em up, futhermucker," prompted by the legend on the boy's T-shirt (FUTHERMUCKER, with some kind of bug-eyed Big Daddy Roth cartoon). Driggers is a genius; he calculates this "innocent" remark of his to enrage the boy, it does, and the boy has the cue ball and draws back to throw it and Driggers has him in a headlock before I can move. Driggers pops him with little uppercuts with the cue ball in the boy's very hand as I manage to wedge him off, which he allows me to do.

"Button your lip, button your coat, let's go out dancing," I say, and he says, "What the fuck you talking about?" and I say, "Mick Jagger," and he says, "I'm just playing pool," smiling the while at the boy and looking at him so intensely the boy stops in his selection of a pool cue and decides not to advance and I buttfuck-waltz Driggers, smiling at everyone, out the door. No one ever advances on Driggers once he is restrained and they see his look, with which he *invites* them to advance on him, pinned. I'd let him go if anyone ever came on, but they don't. Nor does anyone ever bother me, handler of this dog they do not want back on the ground. This is good, because I am a pussy. Driggers is . . . well, Driggers *went*.

Outside, to conclude the fair day, I say, "Driggers, my wife and child have decamped."

"I heard about that."

"I feel like—"

"Make you a better man."

"What?"

"Make you a better man."

"Is that all you got to say?"

"Yep."

And it was. And it was not a bad thing to have said, after I got through formal umbrage, which I thought obligatory. Formal umbrage (and other things) was going to have to go.

"You wouldn't use words like *decamped*, maybe people stick around."

"Is that right?"

"That's right."

"How about *erstwhile*? As in my erstwhile boon companion so totally fucked up from, he says, Vietnam that if he shoots pool someone got to die? Bulldozers erstwhile in *the Nam*—that is so cool, when you guys say that, the de*mon*strative—make him askeert today of bulldozers pushing people's Pampers around?"

"Go ahead. Get it out of your system."

We both start laughing. When I drop him off he says again, "Make you a better man," and slams the truck door. Driggers slams things as a matter of course. Never *put* what you can throw. It's his métier. I put. I tiptoe, whisper. People leave me. Women slide off like snakes. You'd find

Driggers on the floor wrapped up in about a thirty-foot anaconda, calling for his hunting knife, having fun. "She's gone be leaving," he'd say, "but we have to *talk*."

I survey the quiet, my clean floors, still clean. The phone rings.

"What did you mean, 'Mick Jagger'?"

"He wrote that."

"Wrote what?"

"Button your lip, button your coat, let's go dancing."

"How do you *know* this shit?"

"Actually, for all I know, Ron Wood or Keith Richards—I don't know *who* wrote it. Jagger sang it."

"Amazing. Bye."

"Bye."

—

I won't be needing to work so much, and the music can be louder. The balanced-diet shit is out, and NPR. Under every rock is something good if you can scrape off the mold and if the grubs don't scare you into dropping the rock and refusing to move and groove into the New. Skylights may be in order, light shows. Goddamn overhead projector and Jell-O and oil and hippie chicks. The problem is the hippie chicks are younger than my daughter. I need they mommas. They mommas got some sense. Everyone has sense, that is basically the problem I face. I am either behind or too far ahead—so far ahead I bid to lap them. I therefore *look* behind. I'm through with these *sense* fuckers. I'll just run by, run through, forget the baton shit.

New Outgoing Message: Hello, you've reached trouble. If you make sense, I won't call you back. If it makes sense to call you back, I won't. If this makes sense to you, you have the right number. I do not listen to the messages on this machine. As near as I can tell, these machines make no sense. You've called me, uninvited, I am not interested in you or your business; if you are interested in mine, here, take this, my best shot: My floors are clean. And they will remain so.

A bird comes in the house, or *is* in the house. Won't listen to reason, of course. Runs from me. Has been in the house. I did not see it come in. It may have *just* come in, though. I can't say. I can't say a lot of what I am tempted to say, all day. None of us can. I aim to clear some of this up, this presumption, inaccuracy, outright fallacy that governs our days. Clear it all up. Why not. Some new light, new music. Most of the furniture is hers and is de*signed* to burn. Teddy bears on top, beware the burning teddy-bear draft, the noxious gas of child-gone toys going, too.

Call Driggers. "Driggers, do not get downwind of the burning bear. You can *sit* on the goddamn burning sofa, though."

"Shit, I know that."

"You do?"

"Learned 'at first thing in the Nam."

"You fucker."

"You take it easy."

"Roger."

"Wilco."

[*A Piece of Candy*

[**T**attie Elaine McGrim Bolio Pearsall reports, indiscreetly, seeing Robert on New Year's Eve in Ybor City, drunk. She mimics the way he was walking, stiff-chested and aslant and veering and thin-legged, like the Planter's Peanut on a toot, if it is not too hard to imagine the Planter's Peanut getting soused and walking crookedly on those spindly legs, which bend ever lower with each step, while his body takes on the solid-looking heft and bulk of a keg of something which keeps getting closer to the ground. Keeping him upright are his friends Mr. and Mrs. M&M and their new blue baby boy. Mr. and Mrs. M&M are drunk, too, but their new blue baby boy is as sober as a brand-new piece of candy, which is just what he is. Tattie Elaine McGrim Bolio Pearsall, which is not her real name, because I cannot recall her real name, is a bitch, a sweet one, whose reporting of Bobby on the occasion of his perambulating Ybor City like a legally drunk Planter's Peanut is not, I don't think, judgmental. She means no harm by it. She saw it, saw him, she says so, that is all. She is not mean. She is not a bitch. She is a sweet girl of the sort I never knew. I am a hero. She is a sweet girl of the sort I will never know. I will die a hero and she will be a sweet girl of the sort I never knew. As I lie dying a hero I will be able to say she is a sweet girl of the sort I have never known.

I'd like to slap the smile off the face of new blue baby boy M&M, is what I, hero, would like to do. Where precisely does a piece of candy, let alone a new contro-versial—*unproven*—one, GET OFF smirking at an hon-est drunk, even if a young one? Does a piece of candy think it is better than a drunk man? Has it come to this? When in a few years Tattie Elaine McGrim Bolio Pearsall has had the shine knocked off her by Life, when her lipstick's on a little crooked and is a little more or-ange than it should be, or when she has quit lipstick al-together and has shortened her name to McGrim, ha, or maybe to Tattie McGrim, in which case she would be a stripper, or to Paula Bolio, in which case she will be a damned good piece of *prohibito hablar* in these days of Niceness, or to Elaine Pearsall, in which case she will be rich, I would like to have her. That I would like, a hero like me.

I would say, "Pearsall, what say you and I have a bo-lio in the bushes? Could you accommodate a hero with some age on him? What do you suppose has become of Robert Higginbotham?" "Oh, I am so terrible, love," she will say. "If you cannot kiss me, at least pull my hair." I will pull her hair and I will kiss her: I am a hero. Even then will I be a hero. And the new blue baby boy will have been proven, or not, a legitimate piece of candy or an illegitimate piece of shit.

—

Robert Higginbotham was, probably, a gangster. He was not Italian, had no connections, no money, no guns, and no interest in them. He had no silk ties and no tough ways of talking. He had no part in any gang or indeed in any organization. Still, if you looked at him with a relaxed and unassuming mind, even at him bent-legged-drunk veering into the cigar-colored brick walls of the ruined cigar factories of Ybor City, no more than a child, really, and not an unhappy one, what you saw surrounding him was a blue aura of gangsterism, and inside that blue gas of possibility, walking on an invisible circle of quintessentially dangerous potential, was a gangster. Already, smiling, he would instruct you not to call him Bobby. "I will fight you," he would say, smiling. "You may kick my ass, but I will fight you." Smiling.

This is what the woman variously called Tattie Elaine McGrim Bolio Pearsall, Tattie McGrim, McGrim, Paula Bolio, Elaine Pearsall, and Pearsall saw about Robert Higginbotham when she saw him celebrating the New Year in a cigar district gone to boutique and gentrification seed. She saw a gangster and it thrilled her. She was still capable of being thrilled by the not innocent.

As for the man who would call Tattie Elaine Mc-Grim Bolio Pearsall, Tattie McGrim, McGrim, Paula Bolio, Elaine Pearsall, and Pearsall variously a bitch, a sweet bitch, not a bitch, and a sweet girl of the sort he would never know, and never, in the end, have known—

well, of him I can say with certainty only that he is troubled. When he says he is a hero, he is not altogether inaccurate, though he is certainly aware of certain contradictions obtaining between a claim of heroism and the unheroic sentiments coming from the putative hero's mouth, and he is pleased to make no attempt to explain himself, leaving the matter in a small puddle of, he hopes, muddy irony. (And who might I be? you ask. Whoever I am, I do not count. Forget me. Forgive me.)

After the girl Tattie, who will become the woman Pearsall, sees Robert Higginbotham careering into the Ybor City party-down night, she does not see him enter a strip club. There he seats himself, smiling so hugely and whitely that waitresses scramble to get to him first, in the front row of tables before the stage upon which the unsavory revelations will occur. He is thinking specifically of a time in high school when he went to a strip show at the state fair with a group of friends and of one of them yelling "Pork!" and "No more!" at a heavy, aged, admittedly rather unattractive woman who was the first of six strippers in the show. That had embarrassed him. The woman was in fact a sight past unattractive, and his ardent adolescent desire was bent for six weeks into a queer dormancy as a result of seeing her take her clothes off, but she did not deserve to have a boy with acne who would prove homosexual, or anyone else, yell "Pork!" at her. Robert Higginbotham, his desire restored, was smiling tonight partly to make certain he was recognized as the good guy that he was; he was smiling to atone.

From the first scantily clad waitress to get to him he ordered, without deigning look at her, which he deemed unclassy, a drink, and when it came it was turquoise and terrible and cost ten dollars and he didn't know what it was. He drank it and waited for the revelations upon the stage. He had not seen Tattie earlier. He was drunk enough to have strong-armed her in here with him, and Tattie was not yet near being Tattie McGrim, stripper, so it was just as well. Because he'd not seen her and knew nothing of her eminent if brief career to come, doing what he was paying to watch other women momentarily do, he was not sitting there in the Comic Book Club thinking Tattie's absence, or anything else, was just as well. Nothing was just as well to him at that moment. Nothing was just, all was well.

He recalled again the painful adventure at the state fair. The horrific woman, who'd had rolled flesh that swung like wet mop heads, had been the first of six strippers, each of whom improved, sequentially, getting better and better, younger and firmer and prouder, until finally a creature who looked like a hybrid of Marlene Dietrich and an Olympic swimmer took the stage and took the breath out of the boy who'd yelled "Pork!" and "No more!" and took everyone else's breath as well. Robert Higginbotham had been glad to see the boy silenced, and he had been glad to see the beauty of the woman. Her unavailability to him had seemed, for once, correct, and not part of the infinite scheme of torture that was testosterone.

Tonight in Ybor City he got another turquoise drink and still refused to look at the naked woman who brought it to him, and he got ready for the women he was supposed to look at. When they came on it was gratifying that no one was yelling "Pork!" and "Stop!," that no one considered it, that the women were very attractive, that he wasn't surrounded by rubes on sawdust, that he'd bought earlier in the evening some navel oranges, which he now on a whim took two of from the paper sack on the chair beside him and put under his shirt and pushed up into the position of exceptionally high, firm breasts, and he watched the show, every savory and unsavory detail, smiling, and the women were smiling back. They had relaxed and unassuming minds and they saw in the front row, with oranges up his shirt and smiling, a little gangster.

—

Of the hero: of the man who would covet young girls so cannot be a hero: he is morose. He has the power of articulation but nothing of substance, of merit, to articulate. He cannot be a gangster, little and smiling or otherwise; nor can he be an innocent girl who will become a not innocent woman, realistically named or otherwise. He is a *sayer*, a mere sayer.

He is considering—as Robert Higginbotham sits smiling, proffering his proud navel oranges to women mystified by them, and by him—he, the morose, heroic sayer is considering installing on his ample estate a citrus grove. This is the purest of coincidence.

—

Of a coincidence less pure: the fate of a new piece of candy is not easy, nor is the fate of a nice girl. Years later, when Tattie McGrim, who did not know that

Robert Higginbotham the night she saw him drunk in Ybor City would drink turquoise drinks and recall the cruelty of a teenager yelling "Pork!" at a desperate woman, became a stripper herself, what she thought as she looked at herself in the mirror before going onstage was that she looked like pork. "The *other* other white meat," she said, chuckling and pinching a fold of herself. She recalled her mother's insisting pork be cooked until it was hard and dry and white, against the threat of trichinosis. No one worried about trichinosis now. Now it was trichonomiasis, and that wasn't from pork, and cellulite.

She did not, withal, look bad. She was becoming a stripper because, in a roundabout way, her mother's greatest concern in life had been in the neighborhood of holding at bay a disease that had been eradicated forty or fifty years before. She, Tattie McGrim, had suburban ennui. She found insupportable being merely a nice girl with less to trouble her, really, than even her mother had had. She wanted some trouble. It was this wanting, incipient as it was the night she saw Robert Higginbotham acting the Planter's Peanut on a tear, that allowed her to see around his smiling, happy-drunk form the blue aura of a gangster. She was hopeful.

—

That the other women, who did not hope for trouble but already had it and were already stripping for a living, could also see around Robert Higginbotham a blue air of danger is a coincidence, or a contrivance, which is what, universally speaking, a coincidence is.

The universe has conspired that all women who are to come in direct or indirect contact with Robert Higginbotham on New Year's Eve this particular year will see him as a gangster and at some time in their lives take their clothes off in the name of entertainment. If the universe has not actively conspired to effect this improbability, then it has by neglect relaxed its strict grip on probabilities and allowed this rude anomaly obtain. Were Robert Higginbotham to go immediately home from the Comic Book Club, he would find, moreover, his mother stripping for his stepfather, the one time in her life she does it. But he will not go home, because his mother does not know he drinks, and he thinks that the 45-degree angle of his carriage and the bumper-to-bumper pinballing way he's been going through doorways might give him away.

He thinks of the state fair again, not of the embarrassing early part of the show, but of the better, later part. He ate popcorn and it was delicious watching the women. The popcorn was white and hot and savory in his hand, and there were nipples not far away, moving. The world was white popcorn and red nipples. It was delicious, all of it.

Now on his table there are several paper umbrellas, which are served with the turquoise things he's had he doesn't know how many of. If he has all of the umbrellas, he could count them. He has some of the umbrellas, *maybe* all. He cannot ask a naked woman, "Do I have all my umbrellas, or did you take some of them back?" because it would suggest some kind of accusation. He regards the umbrellas he does have and wishes there were

tiny naked women strolling around under them, or reclining and reading tiny paperback books under them
on the table, but his table is too wet for that. He would
not be too abashed to look very closely indeed at the
naked women were they walking around on his table under these fine little bamboo-and-tissue umbrellas. How
lovely must be the East, he thinks, how daintily stupid
and yet somehow *correct*. How undaintily stupid is he
and the West. He takes the stupid oranges out of his
shirt and puts them on the table with the umbrellas.
They look like atom bombs. No one stripping is Asian.
He leaves.

He shoots straight through the door of the club
without hitting either doorjamb and out into the wee
New Year. By now his mother will be through stripping,
for the only time, for his stepfather, which performance
he does not know about and of which performance he
will tell you he does not want to know, and his father, an
airline pilot, will be preparing to strip for his, Robert's,
stepmother, or preparing to do any other untoward
business she might at her tyrannical whim request of
him, Robert's father, which he, Robert, does know
about, the whimsical hoops and his father's sheeplike
jumping through them. They, Robert and his father,
used to go fishing.

———

If stripping for money is valuable as a pursuit of
trouble, of dark anti-suburban anti-ennui, as Tattie Mc-
Grim conceives it, it is because it, stripping—dollar bills
weirdly moist slipped into your string, the emetic wafts

of Scotch and spermine and perfume, and the almost unlimited spectrum of personal problems backstage among the girls, and the interface onstage and just off it with the totally unlimited spectrum of personal problems among the men in front of the stage—stripping is a ground zero for all that is at once crummy and practical in life. Tattie McGrim imagines that the equivalent to stripping for men, remove the sexual component, is being in the lower ranks in the Navy. And maybe you did not need remove the sexual component—all those men on a boat!

In her brief time stripping she saw plenty of Navy boys and they struck her as prototypes of the strip-show goer. They were horny, gullible, loud, not proud, and horny. When you got out of either stripping or the Navy, Tattie McGrim would figure out, you were likely to think of certain kinds of food as "shit on a shingle." This was the essence of the kind of hard, practical, crummy vision of life inculcated by taking your clothes off for money and by being in the Navy. A stripper and a boy in the Navy could actually leave a club together in the early blear of a gray, unpromising morning in modestly eager pursuit of something called shit on a shingle.

—

What kept the hero from wanting the young Tattie Elaine McGrim Bolio Pearsall in a clean, open, lustful way was that he had had, some ten years before meeting her, a daughter. Leaving the hospital that morning, he suffered a difficult divination: that all women were some poor fool's daughter, that he was now one of the poor fools. It was now impossible for him to look at a young woman with desire in his heart and not think of his own daughter, and then, dismissing that frontal assault, he'd suffer a rearguard attack by another idea: that she, any young woman who caught his eye, was someone *else's* daughter. This is but one of the sundry reasons the hero was morose. Desire, once an open honest thing of joyous excess, was now hopelessly pinched and troubled. He had not forgotten how to want; he remembered how to want. He could not want honestly.

The difficult divination that all women are some-one's daughter was reinforced in his brain as he pounded on the locked door of the bar across from the hospital at 11 a.m. The hero was a kind of effete moralist to whom inconvenience was an outrage. The kind of life which led, for example, to people routinely calling food shit on a shingle terrified him. So did pounding on a door lock-ing you out of a drink at eleven o'clock in the morn-ing after you'd seen twenty-six hours of labor and the bloody cantaloupe of a baby girl's head crown. The puri-tans and their inconvenient ways were very much inter-fering with his calmly negotiating with this monstrous discovery that all women are daughters.

He considered leaving the country, this land run by the heirs to ninth-grade class presidents and high-school quarterbacks. This was a favorite idea: living where no one's sense of rectitude would interfere with your lack of sense of rectitude. He had in mind Malay, or somewhere like it so distracted with problems that no one had time for any but his own. He stood at the heavy, chain-beaten door to the bar, with Windjammer written on it by means of a heavy hawser nailed in cursive, and with conch shells stuck to it by means of epoxy, suddenly beginning to wonder: how could he live *where there are women*? He had *loved* women, and now a dark and low and trembling music began to play: he had loved *other men's daughters*. The trash he had talked to people's little girls!

He got in his car and floored it, trying to burn rubber. It had an automatic transmission and wouldn't burn rubber, so he simply left recklessly. It was the best he could do. The moment and its sentiment became, in fact, a kind of motto for the hero from that point on. I have a *daughter*—I do the best I can. But it was clear to him now that whatever one did, with a daughter on earth it was not good enough. Without a daughter on the ground, there was no call to apologize for what you did. With one, what you did would always be merely the best you could do. It would not be good enough. You had blown the *good enough*. You had put a big bet on a big board and a big wheel was spinning and you were not going to win with a daughter in the world and fools like yourself running around after her. The hero, whether he really is a hero or is a hero only in some obscenely, lazily inaccurate sense (forgive me, forget me), had fair reason for being morose.

The door to the bar he pounded on the morning of the daughter revelation never opened, not that day or any other. The building itself was bulldozed shortly before the hero laid eyes on Tattie Elaine McGrim Bolio Pearsall, shortly before she laid eyes on Robert Higginbotham, drunk. The hero had by then stopped drinking.

Young men who had not yet had the vision of daughters could carry on the inebriant tradition, as far as he was concerned.

Robert Higginbotham had not yet had the vision of daughters. In the strip club he pondered, in fact, something of the opposite: how many of the women, he wondered, were *mothers*?

Here is a curious truth with which to leave us: All women are not mothers, but they are daughters all. Through this truth, under its feet as it were, there walks a new blue baby boy, smiling as if he has candy, or as if he *is* candy. You decide, and decide before you father a daughter or mother a boy. It is only the morose, putative hero who wants to slap the boy, whether because he acts as if he has candy or because he is candy. Only the hero is perverse. You are neither, yet, and your responsibilities, which are neither heroic nor falsely heroic, are nonetheless immense.

[*Two Boys*

[Once upon a time there were two boys. They were not boys anymore, actually, one forty-something and one nearly forty years old, but they were not stationed properly in Life as were men their age, and they were not going to be properly stationed in Life. They were not going to be bank presidents or lawyers or own car dealerships. One of them had once momentarily seemed properly stationed in Life for a man of his age; he had been a book editor. But he got into an affair with the editor in chief, under whom he worked, and she was the wife of a gangster who regularly employed the services of hit men, and this, this affair, was a very boyish thing to do. So when the editor resigned and ran, or ran and resigned thereby, he was properly a boy again on the street. He felt better all in all about resuming his true identity except that the stress of having pretended not to be a boy with a gangster's wife who herself knew some of the hit men her husband used had given him cancer of the eyeball. It was his right eye.

The boy with the bad eyeball went through normal hoops trying to not have cancer of the eyeball, second-opinion surfing through waves of options and percentages and knives—

—Not knives, lasers! Why, hold on to that eyeball, in a few years we could save it, if it don't kill you tomorrow—

It will—

No, it won't—

—and then he got done with normal white-coat hoops and rag-bond letterhead and he emerged into a little dungeon where a Chinese woman who spoke only Chinese got ahold of him. "Eye poison in," said the translator he had to take with him. The translator cost more than the Chinese woman who knew how to use the needles and squeeze the earlobes. On the fifth or so visit, well after a man properly stationed in Life would have desisted this quackery, the Chinese woman got down on her knees and thumb-wrestled the boy's earlobe with more than customary vigor and the boy felt what felt like a cord twinging in his head from his ear to the eye in question and then some black stuff began to ooze from the eye in question. "Eye poison out," the translator said, standing at a good remove. The boy was in a marvel of something like not despair. Despair had been when $200,000 worth of lasers and trips to Sloan-Kettering and having a radioactive ingot strapped to his eye in a dark solitary cell for two weeks and chemo nausea had produced only thin bones and hair loss and more coming-and-going white coats and good opinions and letterhead. For $20, black poison had come out of his eye of its own volition. This was more like it, to a boy. When you have an eyeball that is going to kill you, everything is like unto a boy again. Things begin to make original and final sense again, as they did in the beginning before you grew up and got confused. Or got half-confused, as it is proper to say of the forty-year-old boy who has resisted bank presidency. It would be a good thing, for example, after poison has come out of your eye, to go into your tree house and have a meal of chocolate milk and bologna sandwiches and maybe see a good bird. Not much else is required.

—

The other boy, who was a bit older, had also gotten himself tenuously properly stationed in Life for a man of his age, and was also suffering for it. He was a college teacher, a position that is not merely proper but that presumes to look askance at, if not down upon, car dealers and lawyers and bank presidents, but maybe not book editors. The college-teacher boy could not identify what was wrong with him but felt it was something like the other boy's bad eyeball, though larger and vaguer, and he felt it was caused by the same tensions—the strain of posing as a man properly stationed in Life—as had caused the bad eyeball. There was one other link between the two boys: the college-teacher boy's wife was having an affair. She was not having it with a book editor but with a rug merchant. The college-teacher boy wanted to go with the bad-eyeball boy to the dungeon and tell the Chinese woman to make the rugmaker ooze out of his mind, if that's where he was. He was prepared for the Chinese woman to tell him the rugmaker was somewhere else, he didn't care. If she said "Rugmaker in toe" it would be all right as long as she got after the toe. He was prepared to believe in any needles, any herbs, any grains, any tinctures, any thumbholds, any toeholds, any theretofore mystical non-empirical hogwash at all if it would make the rugmaker ooze away back onto the Anatolian plains, where he had frolicked with the college-teacher boy's wife and where he belonged. "She says all trauma is cellular-deep," the boy with the bad eyeball told the college-teacher boy. That would have sounded like an exaggeration in the direction of preciousness to the college-teacher boy before he had begun to have a rugmaker inhabit him. Now it did not sound like hyperbole. It sounded like common goddamn sense.

He felt a little sheepish approaching the Chinese woman with the boy who had an actual bad eyeball when all he had was at most a bad heart or bad head. But the bad-eyeball boy could not see out of his eye, and the college-teacher boy could not think with his head, which rather throbbed, or hummed, but did not *run*. The bad-eyeball boy said, Come on, so they went to the dungeon. If there is anything better than a tree house with chocolate milk and bologna in it, it is an underground fort with a weird woman in it.

—

On their way to the dungeon, the boys stopped to eat. They liked to eat, and they knew a third boy who was also refusing a proper station in Life (though this third boy was not yet in their league as far as absolute dereliction went), who had forsaken a business-management career for a term in the Culinary Institute of America, which allowed him to say "CIA" once or twice a day, and which allowed him to wear a tall hat and call himself a chef and serve food nobody had ever heard of. On the way to the dungeon the two boys had a turkey and onion confit sandwich, chicken sate with yogurt and cumin and turmeric and garlic, a Black Angus tenderloin with an anchiote-seed salsa, and some White Russian ice cream—advanced tree-house food. It fortified them for the underground. If untoward things happened to either of them in the dungeon at the hands of the Chinese woman, they would not prove faint from want of nourishment. In this—eating well and cleaning their plates—they were being quintessentially good boys. They had both figured out, in fact, that it was only in the territory of eating that what was approved of in the behavior of a boy was approved of still in the behavior of a man. They knew women who tolerated obesity because it was a function of, and an unfortunate evil extension to the higher good of, a hearty appetite. A fat guy who cleans his plate was not merely a fat guy. Much of Life came down, in fact, they had discovered, to divining what women expected of you and allowed of you in order to still think of you as a good boy. The bad-eyeball boy said that the Chinese woman was in this sense a kind of purist, if not goddess.

"It's freaky," he said, as they downed the last of their onion confit—they could not figure out what "confit" meant, exactly, but they ate everything—and anchiote salsa. "She takes one look at you and you see her thinking, You have been bad. You have no eat rice I told you. You have not stare at forest. But she does not *ask*, or say anything. She *knows*. It's as if her whole being is attuned to your misbehavior—"

"Well, that *is* sort of her job, right? She sticks needles into the Kewpie doll of your bad ways. She's the Wendy."

"She's beautiful, man."

"Let's *go*."

"Put on your Easter suit. You are going to *church* with your *mother*."

The college-teacher boy thought this a remarkably bright note to come out of the horn of a boy with an eyeball as seriously bad as the bad-eyeball boy's eyeball was bad—a note of great cheer from a possibly dying man. He was seized by a great happy expectation himself. He had no Easter suit, but he took the bad-eyeball boy's meaning and got a haircut and polished his shoes and looked altogether spiffy for their appearance at the dungeon. He had a cottonmouthy shortness of breath which he could not remember having since taking out girls in high school alleged to be willing who weren't.

But the prospect of the dungeon was not sexual so much as it was penal; he regarded the Chinese woman— for reasons not clear to him—as a maternal warden who was going to correct him with benign but iron authority. He thought he might could have used this kind of correction as a young man, at which time the military would have been indicated; now he was older, more ruined, less resilient, more of a slob, when you got right down to it, and the therapeutic forces to right him would have to be subtler than boot camp. He had been a long time away from good mothering. He could not wait. The opportunity to have a good mother who was not your own and who was so expert she could restore you to yourself seemed too good to be true, and in knowing that it was, the college-teacher boy lowered his expectations, or was prepared to, so that whatever she was, as long as she was honest and weird and deft with the needles and the earlobe wringing, she was going to be true enough.

True enough: he was entering the Great Relativity Period of his life. It was the kind of period that if you entered it early you properly stationed yourself, a man, in Life. From the vantage of your law offices or your showroom floor, later, you had no occasion or call to visit a Chinese woman in a dungeon. If you entered the Great Relativity Period late in life, and suddenly accepted or even embraced theretofore unacceptable oxymoronic notions such as Relative Truth, then you looked even more like a boy than you had, proved yourself even less adept at inhabiting law offices (except as a client, perhaps), and had great occasion and call to visit Chinese women in dungeons. The college-teacher boy felt as if he were going to his prom, which he had of course as an inveterate boy not gone to in his time. This was the *ur*-prom, it felt like, and he had the *ur*-date: the head chaperone herself, the great wise corrector. It wasn't black-tie, it was black poison. There was no Purple Jesus to drink in the parking lot; there was green tea to drink in the dungeon. There were no expensive corsages to pin on girls who did not like you. There was a woman going to put pins in your ear who maybe did like you. Things had, withal, improved. The silly prom had become—for the bad-eyeball boy at least, and the college-teacher boy felt there was something deeply (cellular-deep) awry (trauma) in himself as well—a not so silly dance of life.

—

The dungeon was not below grade but it was unofficial enough to count as rebel ground—it was a fort. The Chinese woman was in Western clothes, which made her seem more uncomfortable and more menacing than she would have been in a kimono, if kimono is the right term—it occurred to the college-teacher boy he didn't know one thing Asian from another, not a people or a dress. She reminded him somehow of a jockey.

She greeted them and promptly set to on the bad-eyeball boy, putting a knee in the small of his back and lightly striking the back of his head with something that looked like a ruler for about a half hour. Ordinarily there would have been joking between the boys, but here there was not. It was a profanation even to boys to make fun of a woman looking like a jockey hitting one of you with a stick, seriously purporting to rid you of cancer thereby. It was so preposterous that it could not be a trick, could not be *merely* a woman hitting a boy with a stick. So they watched and felt the Chinese woman beat the bad-eyeball boy with her bamboo-looking splint until the college-teacher boy had time to reflect how similar this business was to a certain boyhood torture called the redbelly, and to notice odd stains on the cheap carpet and not want to allow himself to reflect further on odd stains on the carpet where women redbellied men in the head with a stick, and the Chinese woman was saying something soothing and low with a demonstrative note in it, and in the bad-eyeball boy's ear that was facing up was a black ooze. It was not unlike but considerably less funny than the oil that bubbled up out of the ground when Buddy Ebsen as Jed Clampett shot his land in Appalachia and became a millionaire in Beverly Hills. *An' up thru the ground come abubbalin' crude!* The college-teacher boy was resolutely calmly terrified and sat there resolutely calm to disprove it.

He thought the matter was just beginning, that the ooze would require now a more involved and protracted dealing with the emergency of its emergence, but he was wrong. The woman handed the bad-eyeball boy a tissue and let him up and turned to the college-teacher boy and said, "You." Then she waited. The college-teacher boy looked to the bad-eyeball boy for help, but the bad-eyeball boy merely twisted the tissue in his ear and shrugged.

The college-teacher boy felt eminently foolish and he felt if he talked down to this woman he would deserve to feel foolish, so he let her have it: "My wife is obsessed with another man. She has not become his lover yet, but does not conceal that she would like to. I have offered to facilitate that and get out of the way, but she says no. She dreams about him and writes to him and writes about him. He writes to her. I stand around in the lee of L.U.V. I am not entirely clean. I have hurt my wife similarly, maybe worse. I am due some punishment. I am not a good boy." He looked at the bad-eyeball boy to see if this played any better than it sounded, and the bad-eyeball boy, who was examining his tissue, gave him a thumbs-up, so he continued.

"She can *have* the son of a bitch—he's a 'man of principle' and tall and dark and strange and handsome, and I am none of these, as you can see—" The Chinese woman here blinked very slowly and looked directly at the college-teacher boy, a perfectly inscrutable blink that said either "This is true" or "No, this is not true." He waited for her to intrude with her meaning and she did not. Of course she did not. They had come looking for a good mother, and they had by God *found* one. The bad-eyeball boy had stretched out on the floor for a nap.

"I do not care if the man is in my wife's life. She should have that. Fifteen years of only me is enough for anyone. But I want him *out of mine*. I want this Turk out of my head. He is in it constantly, every waking moment, not in every sleeping moment only because I am too disturbed to dream, I never dream, I would like to dream, if my wife can dream I might deserve to dream myself." The bad-eyeball boy opened one of his eyes and looked at the college-teacher boy as if to comment on the excessiveness of this last speech, and in fact the college-teacher boy had in making it lost some of his resolute calm. He was nervous that in his silliness he had put the woman in a perfect position to do the perfect prototypically mothering thing—"Grow up!"—and for this he need not have come down to the dungeon and witnessed an ear-blackening head redbelly or anything else.

The Chinese woman had unwrapped a cloth roll of needles and showed the college-teacher boy to a chair. The last thing the college-teacher boy managed to say, warily eyeing the roll of needles and allowing the Chinese woman to rather roughly push him into the chair, was "I need a *doctor*." This elicited another thumbs-up from the bad-eyeball boy, who opened neither eye.

The Chinese woman firmly held both the college-teacher boy's shoulders against the back of the straight chair and then released him with a slow, cautionary withdrawing, as if instructing a dog to stay. He stayed. She put one of the needles in her mouth and sat on his lap. He glanced at the bad-eyeball boy, who was apparently asleep. With the needle still in her mouth, the Chinese woman began to trace the contours of the college-teacher boy's face. The needle was so sharp that despite the woman's fine touch the college-teacher boy was certain he would have hairline cuts from the tracing and look like an old china doll when this was over, and this idea, coupled with a sexual nervousness that the woman's sitting on his lap engendered, made him giggle, which he thought would evoke a reproof from the woman, but it did not. She smiled, holding the needle with her teeth to do so, and said, "Git." The college-teacher boy took this to mean "Good."

With the point of the needle the Chinese woman worked his face with such attention to surface that the college-teacher boy, already in a transport of erotic tenderness, could only think of the way he'd once seen overbred beagles work rough terrain for rabbits in a field trial. The dogs were so meticulous, sniffing every pad print of the rabbits, that they made virtually no forward progress. The "best" dog in this venture was the one necessarily the farthest behind his prey. This kind of field trial, in which the game was forsaken for a process itself, was happening on his face.

His face felt sweetly and wonderfully on fire, as if he were bleeding tears. She went on and on. She walked the needle in a crenellation between and around his very eyelashes with such dexterity that he did not even squint. She departed for an ear and he stole a glance at the bad-eyeball boy, who was looking at him with one eye, then the other. He could not recall which of the bad-eyeball boy's eyes was bad, and neither of them looked worse than the other, and there was a tired smile on the bad-eyeball boy's face that suggested he didn't know which eye was bad, or care, either. They had come to a fort with a weird woman in it, and it had worked. The Chinese woman detailed the needle from pore to pore in a way that stung now so badly and agreeably that the college-teacher boy began to wave, in a vision, to his wife. He began to look at the skin of the Chinese woman. He was excited where she was sitting on him, but she acknowledged nothing in this respect. She slowly pulled back and away with the same dog-stay order as before and put the needle back in its roll carefully. The college-teacher boy sat breathing easily, upright, alive, bleeding and weeping without bleeding or weeping, waving happily to his dimming, diminishing wife—it was the way things went. His wife had said of her unforgettable time with her Turk, "It was light, delightful, without promises." But the Turk had kissed her, and there was promise inherent in a kiss, and the Turk would break it, as he, the college-teacher boy, had. He was going to get out of the way of the bull and let the bull break his promise. Without any means of applying those long, colorful barbed darts he could never remember the name of, or of otherwise bleeding the full hump of the bull's exotic lust, there was nothing to do but quit the arena. Capework was silly.

The Chinese woman shifted and was suddenly at his ear with warm breath. She nipped one lobe and crossed before him, brushing him with her hair, which looked fine and black but felt as coarse as broom straw on his face, and nipped the other lobe. She exhaled a long, hot, slow breath in his ear. The college-teacher boy had begun to hold her, to hug her, with what little purchase he had, sitting back as he was. She made no protest or adjustment. He held her still, aware now that he was holding her. She let another hot breath into his ear. Then she said, "You fine."

And he was.